I0458210

Everyone Was Smarter
On Einstein!

Fredric said, "I am one of the committee elected to meet you. It is a pleasure. That coffee smells excellent. I think I shall go to Rosemary's dining room and get a cup."

Ronny and Dorn sat down again and took up their beverages.

Ronny said, "He doesn't sound any more of an egghead than anybody else."

The dog came over and extended his right paw and said to Ronny, "Hello, glad to meet you."

BRAIN WORLD

MACK REYNOLDS

WILDSIDE PRESS

A LEISURE BOOK

Published by

Nordon Publications, Inc.
Two Park Avenue
New York, N.Y. 10016

Copyright © 1978 by Tower Publications, Inc.

All rights reserved

BRAIN WORLD

1

Supervisor Ronald Bronston and Probationary Agent Willy de Rudder of Section G, of the Bureau of Investigation, of the Department of Justice, of the Commissariat of Interplanetary Affairs, snaked over the top of the mountain crest and slid and slipped through gravel a dozen meters to where a rock overhang protected them from being spotted from above. They both wore insulated coveralls, and hoods of the same material, so that facial and physical characteristics couldn't be made out.

Under the ledge, they both slide the straps from over their shoulders and worked the cloth containers to their laps. The containers looked like the sheaths in which fishermen carry their rods.

Ronny Bronston drew forth a plastic telescope. He said, "Winded?"

"Yeah," Willy de Rudder said, and panted. "You know, I never thought we'd make it. Where'd you learn to climb mountains?"

"Back on Earth. Hobby. Mostly in the Swiss Alps, but some in northern India, and some in the Sierra Nevadas, in what they used to call California."

"Why would anybody pick mountain climbing for a hobby?" the other panted.

"Nobody seems to know," Ronny muttered, adjusting the spyglass and leveling it. "The saying goes that you climb a mountain because it is there. Catch your breath, Willy. The way this's been figured, we have twenty minutes to go. By that time, your breathing is going to have to be down to normal if we're going to make the hit."

It didn't take him long to find what he was looking for. "There it is," Ronny said. "Almost exactly a kilometer." He handed the glass over. "Down there on the edge of that little lake."

Willy found the chalet without difficulty. "Holy Ultimate," he breathed in admiration. "That must be the most beautiful setting on Neu Reich."

Ronny Bronston nodded and reached for his container and began to draw objects from it. "They've got a regular fetish about this planet. The planetary engineers they used went all out to attempt to duplicate southern Bavaria. Even imported Earthside flora and fauna."

Willy put down the telescope and pointed. "Look," eh said, excitement suppressed. "Helio-jet."

"It's okay," Ronny told him, attaching a firing chamber to a plastic gun stock. "We figured on them. There's at least two of them in the sky at all times when Number One is in residence at his retreat. But they can't spot us because we're under this ledge, and they can't detect our body heat because of these special outfits, and they can't detect any metal because we haven't got any metal on us, nothing but plastic, pseudo-rubber and cloth. Give me the first section of the barrel."

Willy de Rudder fished into his container and came out with a section of gun barrel about a meter in length. It, too, was of plastic, a very hard plastic. He handed it over and Bronston screwed it into the firing chamber.

"The other one," he said.

Willy handed over another section, then he picked up the telescope and directed it at the chalet again. He said, "He's not out on the terrace yet, but there's a couple of men setting up a table. A table for one. I thought he was supposed to have guests."

"According to our dope, he always eats breakfast alone. And our dope on Number One is accurate. We lost two agents, good men, friends of mine, getting it." Ronny Bronston screwed the second section of the rifle barrel into the first. He reached into his container and brought forth a telescopic sight and slipped it into its groove atop the rifle. "How's your breath coming?"

"Still a little hard. It's partly the altitude."

"We have time. Give me the bipod."

The other brought forth a small two-legged rest from the container beside him and handed it over. Ronny attached it to the end of the two-meter-long barrel and studied out a spot to emplace the weapon.

Willy, at the telescope, said, with an edge of excitement in his voice, "I think this is him."

"No hurry," Ronny said, setting up the odd, ultra-long-barreled gun. He stretched out behind it and peered through the scope. "That's him, all right. Even at this distance you can see how arrogant the funker is. Okay, Willy, it's all yours. How long did you say they checked you out on this product of the Department of Dirty Tricks?"

"About three weeks. I could hit a fly at this range."

Ronny rolled out of the way and took the telescope from the other. "Zero in on him." He directed the plastic viewer on the chalet.

Willy lay down on his belly and got into comfortable position. He got the cross-hairs of his sights onto the body of the man who was just sitting down to the table, far below on the chalet terrace. Three others hovered in the background, obviously flunkies.

He brought a very small screwdriver from a pocket of the coveralls and began very delicately to adjust a screw on the scope's side.

Ronny said quickly, "That's not metal, is it? Once we go on the run, they could pick up any amount of metal at all and especially be suspicious of any that was in movement."

"No. It's a plastic gismo they gave me back at the Octagon."

Ronny grunted, peering through his spyglass. "He's seated facing us. Try to hit him in the chest. It doesn't make too much difference. One hit, anywhere, and we've accomplished what we want. How's your breath?"

"Much better."

"Hold out your hand."

Willy held out his right hand. It didn't tremble.

"Wizard," Ronny said. "But we'll wait another ten minutes to be absolutely sure that you're steady."

For a time there was silence, then Willy said, his voice low, "When I was recruited into Section G I didn't know that my activities would include political assassinations."

"Neither did I, when I was recruited," Ronny Bronston said wryly. "By the way, you weren't recruited, you were suckered in."

The other looked over at him. "How do you mean? I've had the dream of going into space,

10

participating in the expansion of mankind into the stars, since I was a kid. Everything I did, studied, worked at, was with that in mind. I *applied* for a position that would take me into space."

"Ummm," Ronny said, still eyeing the scene on the chalet terrace below. "But Commissioner Ross Metaxa has a few hundred men going around at all times, seeking out potential Section G agents. When they get a cross on one they move in on him and he soon finds out that the *only* chance that he'll get an appointment to get into space is by joining Section G. It usually takes about three years to check you out satisfactorily."

Willy de Rudder was staring at him.

He said, "Why do you tell me that, especially at this time? What you're saying is that I'm not my own man, that I've been maneuvered. And maneuvered into a position I never expected to find myself in. I don't approve of political assassinations."

"Neither do I," Ronny said wearily. "Neither does Section G...ordinarily. This is an exception. Usually, crisping a dictator doesn't do any good. You just get another dictator to take his place and the second one might be worse. I don't know how well you're acquainted with Earth history, but some time ago a radical named Lenin overthrew the government of Russia and became a dictator...of sorts. A member of an opposition party, the Social Democrats, got near enough to shoot him. It took him several semi-invalid years to die from the wound. When he did, another dictator named Stalin took over. The thing is, no matter how mistaken he might have been, Lenin was an idealist. Stalin was a monster. How many millions of deaths can be laid to

11

his hands, we'll never know. Ghengis Khan was a piker."

"Then why is our mission to shoot Number One?"

Ronny looked over at him. "I wasn't in on the decision making. I'm a supervisor in Section G. Policy is made by upper echelons in the Bureau of Investigation. I'm a field man." That didn't sound like sufficient answer to a valid question on the part of a tyro agent, so he added, "I have the dream, the United Planets dream. I take the orders of those who are working it out in detail."

Willy de Rudder said, "But why is Number One, of this planet Neu Reich, any different than the one you mentioned, Lenin? How do we know but that a worse one won't come to power?"

Ronny said, still wearily, "It would seem that he's an exception. You see, Willy, most dictatorships aren't really one man affairs. They're a team. Alexander the Great didn't destroy the Persian Empire and take everything all the way to India; his team did. A team recruited largely, by the way, by his father, Philip, who was a *real* military genius. Caesar too had a devoted team, a competent one. Certainly, Napoleon did. He rallied around him some of the outstanding military, political and even scientific capabilities of his time."

"But Number One?"

"Is unique. It would seem that he alone carries the whole Neu Reich program on his shoulders. Finish him and their dreams of expanding into this section of the galaxy and absorbing other planets—planets now in the loose confederation we call United Planets—would probably go under."

"But not certainly?"

"Few things are certain, Willy. How's your breathing?"

"Almost normal. As an agent of Section G will I often find myself in a position such as this—waiting to murder a man who is in no position to defend himself?"

"I wouldn't know." Ronny Bronston put down the telescope he'd had trained on the dictator below, and turned to his somewhat younger companion. He said definitely, "Willy, all the chips are down now. There's a very good chance that we won't get out of here. Once we hit Number One, the manure will be in the fan. So I might as well check you out now, in all decency, on the full story. If we do get out, you'll no longer be a probationary agent, you'll be a first grade agent—may the Holy Ultimate have mercy on your soul, assuming that there is any such thing as a Holy Ultimate, and I doubt it."

"Go on," Willy said, his voice a little tight. He had taken his eye away from the scope sight, with its victim beyond.

Ronny said, "Let's make it very basic. When under-space was discovered and it became practical for inter-galactic expansion on the part of mankind, things became chaotic beyond belief. Man exploded into the stars like, well, Commissioner Metaxa once called it lemmings. They took off from the mother planet, Earth, in all directions and for every reason known to man nor beast. Political reasons—they wanted a *true* Utopian society, a true Socialist, Communist or perhaps Anarchist society. Or like the Pilgrims of American history, a planet where they could practice their religion without outside interference. In short, go to hell in their own way.

Some went for crackpot reasons such as getting back to nature and giving up all technological progress. All right, so who cared? If a couple of thousand cloddies got together and went looking for an Earth-type world where they could revive ancient paganism, including witchcraft, what business was it of anybody else? A loose confederation, based on Mother Earth, was formed for interplanetary cooperation. United Planets, in short. Willy, what are Articles One and Two of the United Planets Charter?"

The other looked at him, his hood masking his frown. "Why, anybody knows that. Article One: *The United Planets organization shall take no steps to interfere with the internal political, socio-economic, or religious institutions of its member planets.* Article Two: *No member planet of United Planets shall interfere with the internal political socio-economic or religious institutions of any other member planets.*"

Ronny nodded. "Right. And those two articles are the very basis of United Planets. However, there came a new development. Over a century ago one of our Space Forces scouts picked up a derelict, drifting, blasted and burnt out alien spacecraft. It was obviously military in nature, had been destroyed in some interplanetary conflict and it contained the charred remains of a life form—obviously intelligent. It was about the size of a monkey but with a larger head, and it had the equivalent of hands capable of handling delicate tools.

"All of a sudden, the highest echelons of United Planets realized that mankind was in the clutch. No longer could we be philosophical about those

14

segments of our race that were not advancing scientifically, technologically. Sooner or later, man in his expansion into the galaxy, would come up against this intelligent life form, or possibly the other life form with which it had waged interplanetary conflict.

"When our engineers examined that burnt out one-man spacescout, they were scared silly. It was too far gone for them to be able to figure out any of the devices aboard, but they could learn enough to know that the little monkey-like creature was backed by a technology as far ahead of us as we are of Neanderthal man."

Willy said unhappily, "Well, maybe this intelligent alien life form would prove friendly."

"Wizard," Ronny said wryly. "And maybe not. Remember it was a military craft the critter was in and it had been destroyed in a fight. It was obvious that mankind could no longer refrain from progressing in science and technology as rapidly as possible. We could no longer tolerate, in United Planets, worlds with crackpot political, socio-economic, or even religious systems that prevented all-out development.

"So Section G was secretly organized to subvert Articles One and Two of the Charter. By any method found necessary, we pushed the member worlds ahead, even in spite of themselves. If there was a planet with a feudalistic social system, we undermined it and made efforts to establish a capitalistic one, under which progress would be the faster. If there was a dictatorship, where a self-proclaimed elite held up progress the better to milk the man in the street, we subverted it. It there was some religion that held up progress, we undermined it."

Willy de Rudder said unhappily, "Why keep it all secret? Why not just come right out and inform the whole United Planets confederation about these aliens, and urge them to cooperate in all-out advance? The danger is a common one."

Ronny peered through the telescope again, checking the terrace of the chalet. Number One was beginning to eat.

"How's your breathing?" he said.

"Just about normal."

"We'll wait a few more minutes," Ronny decided. "To go on with it, we can't just come out and make a plea for unity in the face of a common potential foe, because there is nothing that man hangs onto more fanatically than his religious, political and socio-economic beliefs. The Christians died in the Roman arenas rather than give up their God. When the advent of the atomic bomb came along, did the United States and Soviet Russia, of those days, unite in the face of mutual destruction? Hell, no. They went into an arms race. *Better dead than Red*, the Americans said, and the Russians had similar slogans. Socio-economics? You get an advocate of capitalism and one of socialism together and they'll argue till hell freezes over before one will give in. No, Willy, we had to do it behind their backs. And that was, and still is, the basic reason for the existence of Section G, though complications have come up recently."

He took a deep breath. "At any rate, that's why we're here on the planet Neu Reich. Number One stands in the way. This world isn't even a member of United Planets and he's rattling his scabbard,

16

threatening to take over some of the other humanity-settled worlds in this sector."

He reached into a pocket of his coveralls and brought forth an odd looking cartridge. It was quite long and even the case was of plastic.

Ronny handed it over. "All right, Willy, this is it," he told the other.

Willy de Rudder took the bullet. He said, "Only one? Suppose I miss?"

"In the first place, you'd never get a chance to get another shot at him. That gobblydygook gun is a single shot deal and he'd be away and into the chalet before you could reload. But besides that, this plastic weapon was designed with only one shot in mind. The barrel is ruined after only one. You'd be hard put to hit *anything* with it. No, we get only one chance."

Ronny took up the telescope again and trained it on the dictator below. Willy snuggled up against the stock of the gawky rifle and brought his eye to the scope.

Ronny said, "Okay. Hit him smack in the middle of the chest. Or, at least, aim for it. That cartridge will do the job."

The long barreled plastic rifle had two triggers. De Rudder pressed the first one, the set trigger, then very carefully brought his finger back to the hair trigger behind. He took a deep breath, held it and gently squeezed. The gun hissed and, in spite of the manner in which the stock was padded, the marksman's shoulder was thrown back.

Ronny snapped, "You missed! Come on, let's get the hell out of here!"

2

They scrambled to their feet.

Ronny Bronston snorted, "I thought you could hit a fly at that distance. Come on, let's go! The fat's in the fire now. It's estimated that he has a thousand security men in the vicinity."

Willy, panting again, said, "The gun? We can't leave it here. Sooner or later they'll find it and possibly be able to trace it to Section G."

"Screw the gun," Ronny said, scooping it up and tossing it out into the open, and the telescope after it. "That's why we were so careful to keep it in light-tight containers. Half an hour in the sun and the plastic it's made of melts away. Same thing applies to the telescope. The only thing they could possibly find are the lenses and they'd have their work cut out tracing them. Bring your container, though. We'll ditch them, somewhere along the way."

They scampered, slipping and sliding in the gravel, up to the crest. There they secured the belaying ropes that they had left there earlier.

Ronny snapped, "It'll take them a while to get organized. No attempt has been made on Number One for years, and they've probably gotten lax. Besides, the gun was silenced. They'll have their jollies figuring out where the shot came from."

Even as he talked, he was roping up, groaning inwardly that the other was a tyro.

"Now, listen," he said urgently. "It's going to be tougher going down than coming up. On the way up, we could take our time and take the easier route. Now, we're in a hurry. It's better to have three men, or even four, on the rope but there's nothing we can do about that. Follow my instructions, no matter how drivel-happy they might seem to you."

"Wizard," Willy said, his voice sounding dry.

"One thing to always remember," Ronny said. "Roped-up, like this, if a man falls and is suspended without foot or handhold, he dies within a few minutes. His organs are squeezed out of place. So, if I'm leading and I fall, get me up, or get me to some place where I can get a hold as soon as possible."

Willy took a deep breath. "Right."

Ronny started off, traversing down, along a ledge.

He called over his shoulder, "Keep an eye open for their helio-jets. There'll be a dozen of them in the sky shortly. Yell if you spot one. We'll have to take cover. They can't heat-detect us, nor detect any metal on us, but they can see us."

"Okay," the younger agent said.

In mountain climbing, you seldom go straight up or straight down. Usually, it's a matter of working your way sideways, traversing, and up, or down, as hand and footholds allow. Ronny led, surefooted. His companion was less so, but largely managed to keep his feet.

Ronny said, "Coming up, we took it the easy way. Going down, we're going to take the stickiest route. For one thing, they probably number comparatively few mountain climbers among them, and there's probably not overmuch equipment for even those, in the chalet and its service buildings. For another, the helio-jets will have their troubles to keep from crashing if they get too low among these gullies, ridges and crests. There's too much air current, down-drafts, up-drafts and so forth."

"All right," Willy said, already puffing at the pace his companion was setting.

They came to a chimney, possibly a meter and a half across and Ronny said, "Here is how you get down this. You press your back against one side, and your feet up against the other and kind of walk down."

He started demonstrating.

Willy de Rudder swallowed. The chimney was at least thirty meters deep. He started after, his fingers mentally crossed. So far, there was no sound nor sight of the helio-jets that were their potential nemeses. Unbelievably, so far as Willy de Rudder was concerned, they got to the bottom of the chimney without a fall.

Ronny tossed his container into a hole. "Ditch yours, too," he said. And, when the other did so, rolled a rock over the two.

They started traversing on a down grade again.

They came to a field of snow, up against the mountain. Willy looked at it in dismay. They'd be black spots against the white as they waded and trudged through it.

Ronny said, "Now watch. This is called *glissading*. It's a sliding and skating sort of thing similar to skiing, but without skis. With the exception of falling, it's the fastest method of descending snow slopes, without skis." He stepped off onto the snow and began sliding down, balancing himself with outstretched arms. Willy brought up the rear, considerably less expertly, but he fell only thrice in the passage.

Ronny said, "Damn it, they'll probably spot our trail in that, sooner or later, but there's nothing for it. Let's go!"

They started down over the gravel again. For a time, the going was comparatively easy.

Ronny said, "Oh, something I forgot to tell you earlier. If one of us is hit, or in danger for other reasons of being snagged, he's got to be finished off. We can't afford to fall into the hands of Number One's boys. You wouldn't want to anyway, but the thing is if they'd put you under Scop, or whatever truth serum they use on Neu Reich, you'd spill it that you represented Section G. So if anything happens to me, finish me; I'll do the same for you. If both of us are in danger of being snagged, suicide. Damn it, we should have brought cyanide pills."

"Suicide?" Willy said blankly. "How?"

"Holy Ultimate," Ronny said in irritation. "Jump off a cliff or something. Improvise. Oh, oh."

"What's the matter?" Willy panted.

His superior pointed. Possibly three kilometers off, easily discernible in this clear mountain air, was a group of five or six uniformed men. They were roped together and all bore alpine sticks, with flak guns slung over their shoulders. They were ascending the mountain by approximately the same route the two Section G operatives had earlier in the day.

"They haven't spotted us yet," Ronny growled. "Double damn. I hadn't expected to be flushed this early in the game."

"What do we do?" Willy panted.

"Head back this way. We'll get this ridge between

21

them and us. With luck, they'll get all the way to the top before they head down again after us. See that dog?"

For the first time, Willy de Rudder saw the dog. It looked half the size of a nearly grown calf, was unleashed and gray in color.

"It's a kind of Weimaraner that they've bred up on this god-forsaken planet," Ronny growled. "They're better bloodhounds than bloodhounds are. Come on, let's go. How are you making out?"

Willy took a deep breath and got out, "The pace is a little heavy in this altitude, but okay."

"Damn it," Ronny snorted. "That funker Sid Jakes should have given you some time at high altitude and in mountain climbing before sending us on this assignment."

Willy spotted a helio-jet. "Aircraft," he snapped.

They took refuge in a small cave.

Ronny Bronston, beginning to breath somewhat deeply himself by this time, said, "We've got to get down faster. They're already beginning to swarm. I hope in the name of the Holy Ultimate that they don't have another party coming up by this route. If they have, we've had it. Have you ever done any roping-down?"

"I don't even know what you're talking about," Willy panted.

"All right. It's a little scary the first time you do it. Against all your instincts. But it's the fastest way of getting down a mountain."

They came to a cliff. Ronny began untying the rope about his waist.

Willy looked over, cautiously. "Holy Ultimate," he said. "It must be a hundred meters down." He stepped back a distance.

"Not really," Ronny told him. "We don't have enough rope for that. Now here's what we do. They call it *abseiling*, or roping-down. I belay you from up here, you pass the other rope over one thigh and over the opposite shoulder. You back down over the side of the cliff, your feet braced against the cliff wall, and you walk backward, slipping the rope as needed all the way to the bottom."

"Are you kidding?"

"No." Ronny roped him up, continuing directions. "You're in no particular danger. I'm up here belaying you. I've got hold of you all the way down."

Willy's pale face couldn't be seen through the hood, but he said, "I've got a fear of heights."

"So has practically everybody else who's normal. Let's go." Ronny continued to rope the other up in the prescribed manner.

Willy said bitterly, "What do they pay a First Grade Section G agent?"

And Ronny said, completing his servicing of the other, "Five hundred interplanetary credits a month—particularly when he's so well trained that he can hit a fly at a kilometer's range. Come on!"

Willy de Rudder said, "How do you get down? Who belays you from above?"

"You'll see. Get going, Willy."

The younger agent went to the side of the cliff, turned his back, closed his eyes and started down, walking backward, the comforting feel of the belaying rope holding him tight against falling.

It took a million years for him to reach the canyon bottom below.

"Untie," Ronny yelled down.

He untied the rope from around his waist and looked up as Ronny retrieved it. Shortly, the other, the rope doubled, started down, bouncing down the cliff, kicking against it and jumping so that his pace was three or four times that of Willy walking down.

When he got to the bottom, next to his companion, he gave a jerk at one end of the doubled rope.

"Slung over a rock projection," he explained.

The other looked at him. "Suppose you got in trouble, with nobody, uh, belaying you from above?"

"That's a good question," Ronny said. "Come on, let's go. We've got to find more sheer cliffs."

For another period the going was easier again, though they had to duck under another ledge for a time as a helio-jet passed over.

In the cave, the younger agent said, after looking at his companion from the side of his eyes, "Ronny."

"Yeah?"

"I'm sorry about missing Number One. I fouled up the whole project and you said that two agents were lost setting it up."

Ronny Bronston grunted amusement. "Don't let it worry you. We accomplished what we were sent to do. It would have been more fun if you'd hit him dead center. It probably would have taken him a couple of days to get rid of the stench. But you hit the wall immediately behind him and about ten centimeters to the right. That'll do it."

The other came to an abrupt halt. "What are you talking about?"

Ronny chuckled and said, "Section G doesn't condone assassination, even when called for. If it did, and the information ever got out, member worlds of United Planets would drop out like

24

dandruff. That was a special cartridge you fired. The head was filled with the most nauseating odored fluid you ever smelled—especially whomped up in the laboratories of our Department of Dirty Tricks. At impact it was meant to shatter and sprew the smell, a few dozen times worse than a skunk's scent, all over the place. You'd need a gas mask to be on that terrace now. The fluid was otherwise harmless."

"But ... but *why?*"

Ronny left the sheltering ledge and led the way, resuming the bent kneed stride of the mountaineer. "Come along," he said. "Because now he knows he's vulnerable. If somebody could get in through his defenses to a point near enough to shoot a stink bomb shell right next to him, then the next time they could make it something more deadly. He's going to think twice, at least, before he makes any warlike moves. There's another angle too, from Section G's viewpoint."

They had arrived at another cliff and Ronny began ordering the ropes for *abseiling*.

"What's that?" Willy said, no tremor in his voice at what was to come, this time.

"He's got his people all keyed up for his military venture. They've been sacrificing, building munitions plants, a space fleet and so forth, for years. The whole planet is on edge with this scheme to subjugate some of the nearby worlds. If he calls it off, they'll be up in arms against him. And he probably will, since now he knows that if he makes an aggressive move, he'll be hit. No, I wouldn't be surprised to see an overthrow of Number One before the year is out."

In all, during the next three hours, they roped-down four cliffs. Willy de Rudder got quite nonchalant about it, even attempting to duplicate his companion's method of bouncing his way down. Several times they saw helio-jets, but Ronny had been right, the craft were afraid to come too low due to the treacherous mountain air currents. Twice, they spotted groups of uniformed men, obviously searching for them. However, Ronny seemed to be a more competent mountaineer than any of the foe. They were able to keep from being detected.

They were nearly to the small green valley which was their immediate destination when they were flushed by Number One's gray clad security men. The others, a group of four, were possibly a hundred meters away, but the two Section G men were clearly in sight.

"Run for it," Ronny rasped and the two doubled over in that position men assume in combat when under fire, to present as small a target as possible, and dashed. Various weapon fire splashed off the rocks about them.

They zig-zagged in evasive action, got around an outcropping of rocks which afforded immediate protection.

Ronny got out, "They're at least as tired as we are. They've been coming up hill, while we've been coming down. They're undoubtedly short of breath and they're overly excited about spotting us. So come on, let's get out of here, Willy."

From the side of his eyes, the tyro agent could see that his superior was holding his side.

"You're hit," he blurted, scrambling after the other.

"Yeah," Ronny got out. "Come along. If we can

26

make the valley and across it to the trees, we're comparatively safe."

They sped, as best they could, toward the valley. Behind them there were shouts and more weapon fire, though obviously the others were blasting away without target, possibly in an attempt to frighten the quarry into surrender.

"If this squad has one of those damned dogs, we've had it, even if we do make the trees," Ronny gasped.

Their luck held and they managed to temporarily shake the pursuers. However, neither of them had any illusions. The security men would be equipped with two way radio and in short order every search group in the vicinity, and every helio-jet, would be zeroing in on them.

They got to the valley, dashed across at its narrowest point and ducked into the trees of the forest beyond. They stopped for breath, fifty meters into the woods, both leaning their backs against the trees.

Ronny thought about it a deep breathing minute, then said, "Willy, you're going to have to finish me. That hit I took removed enough of my side to construct Eve."

"Finish you!" the younger man blurted.

"Yeah. I'd never make it and we can't take a chance on their getting me alive."

"I'll bandage you up. It's only a little ways to the clearing now."

"Bandage me with what?" Ronny panted.

"With our shirts," the other insisted. "We're both wearing white shirts under these coveralls."

"Wizard, but the moment we get out of these insulated coveralls the helio-jets pick up our body heat. You're going to have to finish me."

"I can't," Willy said. "I...I don't even have a gun—or a knife."

Ronny sighed and took a deep breath. "Use your belt and garrot me. Better still, pick up one of those stones and bash my head in, it'll be quicker."

"I won't do it! We've got less than half a kilometer to go and there'll be a doctor in the landing craft. Here, put your arm over my shoulders. I'll help you."

His superior sighed but obeyed orders and they took off again, from time to time stumbling in the underbrush or over roots. Behind them, they could hear the crashing of others in the woods.

Ronny finally groaned, "Can't make it any further, Willy. Finish me and save yourself. It's necessary to get the message back that our mission was successful."

"Come *on*, Ronny. We can make it. It's no distance at all now."

But Ronny Bronston shook his head, in exhaustion. "No. Finish me. I'm on the verge of fainting. That's an order, Agent de Rudder."

The younger man ignored him, stooped suddenly and took his superior up and slung him over his shoulder and began staggering through the trees.

Ronny Bronston said nothing and the tyro agent assumed that he had passed out from loss of blood. The crashing sounds from behind were louder, now that his pace had slowed, but at least there was no baying of dogs. He doubted that those behind were much in the way of woodsmen. Few were, these days. He doubted that any of them were much good at tracking, unless they were able to use their heat or metal sensors. And those didn't apply to Willy and Ronny.

He tried to move as quietly as possible so that the pursuers wouldn't get his direction from the sounds of his progress, but he was no more the woodsman than they were and he winced at the noise he was making.

Willy de Rudder broke through into the clearing before he had actually expected it.

He stood at its edge and stared unbelievingly. The clearing was empty. "Holy Ultimate," he groaned, "they're not here!"

3

But with a *whoosh* a space landing craft descended like a beam of light and set down within feet of him. The hatch banged open immediately and Willy de Rudder staggered toward it, his companion still over his shoulder. He dumped his load into the small spacecraft, and climbed into it behind him.

Lee Chang Chu was at the controls, her almond eyes slightly wide. "What's happened?" she snapped, even as she flicked buttons and dropped levers. The hatch slipped shut and they were airborne.

Willy panted, "Ronny took a hit. He's either fainted, or dead."

Lee Chang called over her shoulder, "Doc, quick!" But the medic was already making his way forward, clumsily, through the seats of the landing craft.

The two men wrestled their fallen colleague back into the interior of the small spaceship and stretched him out on the aisle.

Ronny opened his eyes and said weakly, "Take it easy, you funkers. I'm a sick man."

Lee Chang Chu slumped in her pilot seat, in relief.

The doctor zippered the wounded man out of his insulation suit, and began to examine the wound. It was a bloody mess.

Willy staggered erect and said, "I've . . . I've had it. I'm going to puke."

"In the back," the diminutive Chinese woman said. "There's a small head there."

He staggered toward the rear.

The doctor looked at Ronny Bronston and scowled. He said, "You're not hit as bad as all that."

"I know," Ronny said. "But don't let de Rudder find it out. It'd hurt his feelings."

When Willy came reeling back from the small rest room, he had already removed his hood and insulated suit. He was a good looking type, in an overly earnest sort of way. Only average of weight and build, he didn't look as though he could have carried a limp man, as heavy as himself, half a kilometer through heavy woods while already in a state of exhaustion. He also didn't look like a cloak and dagger type.

Lee Chang Chu, though not knowing what game Ronny had in mind, played along. She said, "Come up here, de Rudder, and give me a rundown, while the doctor is patching up our Ronny."

The tyro agent was glad to. Besides, he knew that the Chinese woman was of supervisor grade, as was Bronston, so he was under her command. He sank into the seat next to her in weary relief.

Section G Supervisor Lee Chang Chu was small, almost tiny. She looked to be at least three quarters Chinese, or possibly Indo-Chinese, the rest European or North American. She favored her Oriental blood; her silk dress was traditional Chinese, slit almost to the thigh on each side. She was delicately pretty, with only a touch of the Mongolian fold at the corner of her eyes. On her it looked unusually good. Her complexion was that which only the blend of Chinese and Caucasian can give. Her figure, thanks to her European blood, was fuller than Eastern Asia boasts; tiny, but full.

She said to the probationary Section G operative. "How did it come out?" Her voice was small but very earnest, a no-nonsense voice. She was the most unlikely looking secret agent possible, but one does not achieve to the rank of supervisor in Section G without the necessary ability.

He said, hesitantly, "Evidently satisfactorily, according to Supervisor Bronston."

She looked over at him questioningly. "Evidently?"

"Yes. I missed but the bullet exploded only a very short distance behind him. I assume that he was probably splashed with the stench."

She tinkled a laugh. "I would have loved to have seen that stern face of his when the smell hit him." But then she looked at the other again. "Missed him? With *that* gun?"

"Yes."

She threw a lever and they left the atmosphere of Neu Reich and went into space.

She said, "We'll rendezvous with the Space Services Scout within ten or fifteen minutes."

Willy de Rudder said, "I'm not much up on these things. This is my first trip overspace. But won't Number One's spaceship get after us?"

Lee Chang Chu smiled. "No. We have gismos that prevent them from getting us in their sensors. Our spy Space Scouts are almost impossible to detect, at any distance at all, especially with the facilities of comparatively backward planets such as Neu Reich."

It was his turn to look puzzlement at her. "I thought that Neu Reich was up on the list of planets with a high military potential. I thought that was why we were upset about her."

She shook her head and said, "That is one of the things you must keep in mind about dictatorships, Willy... I assume I may call you Willy. You saved Ronny's life and I am very close to him."

"Of course, Supervisor Chu."

"Lee Chang," she said. "We're very informal in Section G. We have to be. Too often our lives are dependent upon the agent next to us. At any rate, dictatorships have an Achilles heel. On Neu Reich, their most brilliant space specialist, I supoose you could call him, was a chap who was far and away in advance of the scientists on most either planets. His name was Richthofen, which is about as Germanic a name as you can get. However, some cloddy or other—but not from our viewpoint—put his lineage on the computers and, surprise, surprise, about ten generations ago, space scientist Richthofen turned out to have had a Jewish ancestor. He escaped the planet by the skin of his teeth and refugeed to Earth. We obtained his services. We are now capable of negating the detection sensors of Neu Reich, mainly though his efforts."

"I see," Willy said. "You know, two or three years ago I had no idea that such a department as Section G even existed. Now I am continually amazed at its ramifications."

She smiled ruefully and on her it came out like a dream. She nodded and said, "That applies to 99 point something percent of the human race—and must. We don't seek publicity, Willy."

Ronny was bandaged and had several hypodermic shots in him by the time they rendezvoused with the Space Forces Scout. He was groggy from the drugs and seated comfortably near the rear of the landing craft. They settled into the hatch which housed their small spacecraft in the scout without a hitch. Lee Chang Chu was an expert pilot.

As soon as she had opened the hatchway, the two men got Ronny up and wrestled him through it as gently as possible. Lee Chang brought up the rear.

The captain was awaiting them in the corridor of the scout. His eyes went anxious and alert when he saw Ronny was wounded.

Lee Chang said briefly, "We've had a casualty. Put him into a bunk. Then let's get into under-space. Sheer bad luck might bring us up against one of Number One's space cruisers."

"Yes, ma'm," the captain said, touching the visor of his cap. He called over his shoulder. Two spacemen came up and took Ronny gently. The captain hurried for his bridge.

By the time they reached the Neuve Alburquerque spaceport, the wounded man was well on the road to repair. The three Section G agents made their farewells to the doctor and the crew of the space scout and took a passenger craft to the Greater Washington shuttleport. There they separated, Ronny heading for his apartment for a night's rest, fresh clothing and a few drinks before reporting in to the Octagon in the morning.

The next day, he scowled down at his bandaged waist and wondered whether or not to remove the dressing, but decided not to. It wouldn't hurt to keep

34

it on for another couple of days.

He took an automated helio-cab from the pickup point on the roof of his apartment house and dialed through to the Octagon, that city within a city on the other side of the Potomac. At the sixth gate, he got out and dismissed the vehicle.

He approached one of the guard-guides, brought forth his wallet and flicked it open to reveal his badge. It was golden, had a queer sheen and read simply *Ronald Bronston, Section G, Bureau of Investigation, United Planets*. The guard was a stranger, big and obviously proud of his uniform which he wore with a swagger.

He scowled at the badge and said, "Section G? Never heard of it."

Ronny looked at him and said wearily, "It's not necessary that you have heard of it."

The other took him in. Ronny Bronston was a man of averages. Medium height, medium weight and breath. Pleasant enough of face in a medium sort of way, but not handsome. Less than sharp of dress, hair inclined to be on the undisiplined side. Brown hair, dark eyes. In a crowd, inconspicuous. He didn't stand out.

The guard said, "Where's your pass?"

"I don't need a pass. I'm a supervisor of Section G."

"You need a pass to get by me, friend."

Ronny decided that it was going to be one of those days. He said, "Look here, who's your immediate superior?"

The officious one scowled at him. "Lieutenant Economou."

"And who's his immediate superior?"

"Commander Hersey."

"And who's his immediate superior?"

"General Wayne Fox, Commander in Chief of Octagon Security."

Ronny Bronston took his badge and put it in the slot of the Tri-Di phone screen standing next to the guard's post. He said, "General Wayne Fox."

The guard's face went suddenly empty.

When the general's face faded in, he said, "Ronny! I thought you were off on one of those romps of yours."

The guard's face was wan now.

"Just got back," Ronny said. "What do you say we get together for lunch, Wayne? I've got a funny story to tell you about old Number One on Neu Reich."

"Great," the general grinned. "Meet you in the senior officer's mess at noon."

"It's a date." Ronny flicked off the phone screen and turned back to the guard. He said, "Summon me a three-wheel scooter."

The other snapped him a salute. "Yes, sir. Right away, sir." He pushed a button.

When the vehicle came scurrying up, Ronny gave him the coordinates of his destination and the other dialed them hurriedly.

Without a further glance at the man, the Section G operative climbed into the bucket seat and the scooter slid into the Octagon's hall traffic and began proceeding up one corridor, down another, twice taking to ascending ramps.

He shook his head at his run-in with the guard and actually felt a bit ashamed of the cavalier manner in which he had handled the man. What was it about

36

third-rate people in positions of minor authority?

He must have traveled three kilometers before they got to the Department of Justice alone. It was another half kilometer to the Bureau of Investigation. The scooter eventually came to a halt, waited long enough for Ronny to dismount and then hurried back into the hall traffic.

Ronny entered the office. There was a neatly uniformed reception girl-cum secretary there at the sole desk the room boasted. She had a harassed and cynical eye, was evidently about forty, and looked ultra-efficient, rather than good-looking. She was widely thought of as the operational brains behind Section G, and she was also reputedly sugar on Ronny Bronston.

Ronny said, "Hi, Irene. What's the jetsam today?"

"Ronny!" Irene Kasansky said, never ceasing for a moment in the flicking of levers and pushing of buttons, "We heard you were shot in that Neu Reich assignment. Shouldn't you be in bed?"

"It wasn't as bad as all that. I came to report. Maybe afterwards I'll ask for some time off to rest and go fishing. Is Sid in?"

She clicked an order-box and spoke into it, listened for a moment and then said, "If I wasn't a lady, I'd clobber you, you idiotically grinning cloddy."

She looked up at Ronny. "He's free."

"Thanks, Irene," Ronny said and went through the door behind her. He made one turn to the left and two to the right, in the corridor that stretched beyond, and came up to a door lettered simply, *Sidney Jakes.*

He knocked and a voice called happily, "Come on

37

in, come on in. It's always open."

Ronny entered and found Sid Jakes behind his desk. He was the most off-beat looking high government executive that Ronny Bronston had ever met, Assistant to Ross Metaxa, Commissioner of Section G. His dress was on the ultra-informal side, seemingly more suited to sports wear than a job in the super-conservative Octagon. He couldn't have been much older than Ronny's thirty or so and he had a nervous vitality about him that could wear another down in a matter of half an hour.

On Ronny's appearance, he popped to his feet and dashed about the desk to wring the newcomer's hand with an enthusiasm that would have suggested they were long separated brothers. "Ronny, old chum-pal," he said. "My right arm!"

"Thanks, Sid," the newcomer said sourly. "You keep giving me these sticky assignments and I'll probably have my own shot off one of these days."

"Sit down, sit down, old chum-pal," Jakes said. He rushed his subordinate to a chair, saw him seated, then dashed back around the desk to his own swivel chair.

He said, his voice the nearest to sounding serious that it ever got, "Lee Chang reported that you copped one on Neu Reich. How come you're up and around?"

Ronny shook his head. "It wasn't much of a hit. I faked most of it to see how Probationary Agent Willy de Rudder would react. I pretended to be so badly hit that I ordered him to finish me off, so I wouldn't fall into Number One's guards' hands."

The other cocked his head. "How did de Rudder

work out? He looked like he had the makings of a pretty good agent."

Ronny made a negative motion with his right hand. "He's not field agent material, Sid."

His superior said, "Why not?"

"First of all, he missed Number One. And he did it on purpose, though he was under direct order to shoot the funker. Evidently, he couldn't bring himself to kill an unknowing, defenseless man."

Sid Jakes didn't get it. He said, "That gimmicked up bullet wouldn't have killed him. Especially in view of the fact that we know he wears bulletproof underwear, or whatever, all the time."

'I know. But I didn't tell de Rudder that until later. I wanted to see how he'd react, how dedicated a Section G agent he would make."

"And then?"

"Later I pointed out to him that if one of us was in danger of being snagged that the other would have to finish him off. Or if both were in such danger that we'd have to suicide. Some time after, I took a minor hit, but pretended it was much worse. I ordered him to garrot me with his belt, since we had no weapons. He refused and insisted on helping me back to where Lee Chang was scheduled to pick us up. Finally, I told him I was going to faint and gave him a direct order to finish me. He still refused."

Sid Jakes got out a happy laugh. "Suppose he'd have obeyed the order? That would've been a neat trick on you if he'd done it."

Ronny shook his head. "If he had started to, I would have recalled the order and proceeded on to the rendezvous point on my own two feet. He's not field agent material, Sid. He's too emotional, too sentimental."

Sid Jakes grinned at him. "Ronny, he was trying to save your life."

Ronny looked at him emptily and said, "Under the circumstances, Sid, at that time, that supposedly wasn't the requirement."

Sid Jakes flicked on his order box and said into it, "Sweetheart, assign former Probationary Agent Willy de Rudder to some desk job here at headquarters."

The box squawked back and he grinned and said, "All right, all right, but if your disposition doesn't improve I'll withdraw my proposal of marriage."

He flicked the orderbox off and laughed amusement and said, "What a woman. I'll wager she drinks vinegar with her meals instead of wine. If she wasn't so indispensible, Metaxa would have fired her years ago. As it is, you're the only one in the Bureau she doesn't climb all over."

4

The phone screen lit up and Ross Metaxa was there. As usual, he looked rumpled, tired, and as though he'd had too much to drink, or too little sleep, or both, the night before. The Commissioner of Section G was in his middle years, sour of expression and disposition, moist of eye, dark of complexion, as though he was of Mediterranean extraction.

He said now, "Irene tells me that Ronny is there with you. How did the Neu Reich assignment come off?"

Sid Jakes chuckled. "You know Ronny. Never fails. But we had to scratch that probationary agent we sent with him."

"All right. Don't bother me with the details. Both of you come to my office. I've got another job for Ronny."

Sid said, "He's recuperating from a wound."

"Can he walk?"

"Sure. As Irene told you, he's here in my office."

"Then come on over." The weary face faded.

Sid Jakes shook his head. "The Old Man's a goddamned slave driver. Maybe we can talk him out of it." He came to his feet and led the way.

Ronny sighed and followed. Damn little chance there was of ever changing Ross Metaxa's mind about anything.

They went down the hall to a door inconspicuously lettered *Ross Metaxa, Commissioner, Section G.* Ronny wondered all over again at the lack of ostentation in all pertaining to this man, who was possibly the single most powerful figure in United Planets, all unbeknownst to the billions of persons who counted themselves citizens of the loose confederation.

Sid Jakes knocked briefly and pushed on through followed by his top agent, without waiting for response.

Metaxa was behind the desk. On their appearance, he opened a drawer and brought forth a squat dark bottle and a glass. "Drink?" he said, pouring a heavy shot.

"At this time of day? And that?" Sid Jakes snorted. "I'm much too young."

Ronny made with an exaggerated wince. "Denebian tequila," he said. "I wonder what the hell they make it out of."

Metaxa knocked the water-colored guzzle back over his tonsils with the stiff wrist of the practiced drinker.

He said, "Sit down. How bad's your wound, Ronny?"

"Not too bad. I'll be taking the bandage off in a couple of days. However, I *was* looking forward to a vacation."

"It'll have to wait. But this assignment will be the next thing to a vacation."

Sid Jakes chuckled, "I'll bet."

Ronny said in resignation, "What's it all about?" The newcomers had taken seats.

But at that moment came another knock on the

42

door and Ross Metaxa pressed a button beneath his foot to activate it.

There entered possibly the largest man Ronny Bronston could ever remember having seen. His size was considerably muted, however, by his ultra-conservative dress, the anachronistic pince-nez glasses he wore, and his air of the scholar. It was Doctor Dorn M. Horsten. All three knew him, though he and Ronny hadn't been in contact since the noted research algae specialist had been recruited into Section G.

Ronny and Sid Jakes came to their feet and shook hands and exchanged the usual amenities.

Metaxa growled, "Sit down, everybody." He looked at the big man. "You're the least likely seeming agent in the section. I understand that Lee Chang Chu recruited you into her Special Talents class, as she calls it. ESPers, midgets, pickpockets and everything else off-beat. What's your special talent?"

Doctor Horsten was a very nice, very soft-spoken man. He said, "I suppose that the best thing would be for me to demonstrate."

He brought forth from its shoulder rig his H-gun. In his hands the large weapon was dwarfed. He took the barrel and twisted it into the shape of a pretzel.

The Section G Commissioner bug-eyed him. "You can't do that!" he said indignantly.

Dorn Horsten said mildly, "Yes, I can. The standard prejudice that double-domes, as the expression goes, don't have muscles fails to stand up on my home world of Brobingnag, Commissioner. You see, we have a 1.4 G planet. On top of that, the

43

original colonists, from Scandinavia, were, ah, nature boys, I believe is the usual term of disapprobation. At any rate, I would wager than Brobdingnag produces the strongest citizens in United Planets. Besides that, since boyhood I've made a hobby of weight lifting and, ah, doing such things as tying knots in one-inch mild steel bars."

"Wizard," Metaxa sighed. "Happily, you won't be needing your special talent on the brainworld. This assignment is purely routine."

"Brainworld?" Ronny said.

"Einstein," Metaxa said, looking over at him. "Ever heard of it?"

"I don't believe so. Wasn't Einstein a prominent physicist of the 20th Century?"

"I've heard of it vaguely," Dorn Horsten said. "I met one of their scientists, a brilliant chap, at a conference on the phylum *Thallophyta* on the planet Firenze some time ago."

Metaxa nodded. "He'd be brilliant all right, if he came from Einstein."

"Member of the United Planets?" Ronny said.

His superior shook his head. "No. That's why we're here. They just applied for membership."

He took up his bottle of tequila and poured himself another slug and gestured with the bottle in way of offering to Horsten.

Doctor Horsten shook his head. "I've heard about your tequila," he said mildly.

Metaxa knocked the drink back and said, "Let me give you some background. When Einstein was first colonized, some time ago, there was one big basic requirement demanded of the colonists. Aside from

44

good physical health, they had to have an I.Q. of at least 130."

"What's I.Q.?" Ronny said.

"An early method of measuring your Intelligence," Sid Jakes told him. "That's a neat trick. Populating your world with double-domes, as Dorn calls them."

Metaxa said, "Briefly, this is how it works. It was the French psychologist Alfred Binet who created, in 1904, the first systematic intelligence tests. Quite a few variations came along later. Here's the general idea."

He picked up a paper from his desk and began to read.

"Intelligence tests consist in general of a heterogeneous series of questions to be answered, problems to be solved, and tasks to be fulfilled, all of varying degrees of difficulty, which the individual is given to complete within a specified time. The questions and other parts of the test mean nothing in themselves, and so-called standardization of the test is essential before any conclusions as to intelligence can be drawn. Standardization of a test consists in its administration to as many individuals as possible of various ages. From the results thus obtained it is possible to determine the average number of questions answered, problems solved, and tasks completed of individuals of certain ages. For example, of 100 questions, the average answered correctly by a child of 7 might be 10; by a child of nine, 15; by a child of 12, 30; and so on. If then a child of nine answers thirty questions correctly, he is classed with the children of 12 and his mental age is said to be 12. The so-called Intelligence Quotient is a comparison between this mental age and his real or chronological age, in this case 9. It is computed by dividing the mental age, 12 by the chronological age (9) and multiplying the result by 100 to eliminate the decimal point. In this case the I.Q. comes to 133, which is relatively high. As the child grows, the mental age and the chronological age generally increase at a relatively equal pace so that the I.Q. varies to only a small extent."

Metaxa looked up. "Most of the I.Q. tests used one hundred as the average, and it was found that the overwhelming majority of persons fell between 90 and 110. Comparatively few were below that, comparatively few above. 100 to 110 was considered to be Above Average; 110 to 120 was considered Very Intelligent; 120 to 130 was considered Superior; 130 to 140 was considered Very Superior; and above 140 was considered Gifted. Some of the tests considered above 160 to be Genius."

Dorn Horsten demured mildly. "That's a somewhat elastic term," he said. "We shouldn't confuse genius with high I.Q. It is usually, though not always, that a genius is very intelligent, but more is needed than that. A subtle something thus far never defined. In fact, the spark of genius can sometimes, especially in the arts, be found in persons of quite mediocre I.Q. It is debatable, for instance, that Edison had an exceptional I.Q. Fairly high, most likely, but not exceptional. When he got out of his own field and commented upon such matters as politics and economics, he seemed a veritable idiot."

Sid Jakes said, "An indication of rating is to be found in the fact that the United States military at the time of the Second World War demanded an I.Q. of at least 110 for entry into OCS, the officer's training school." He chuckled. "Another indication is that at one time the U.S. Army decided that no man could hold sergeant's rank unless he had an I.Q. of at least 90. So they gave all the sergeants an I.Q. test and so many of them failed to make 90 that they had to give up the requirement. They wouldn't have had any sergeants left."

"All right, all right," Metaxa said impatiently. "But to get back to the point. Since being first colonized with Earthlings with Very Superior I.Q.s, or more, Einstein has evidently made a policy of upgrading their average intelligence."

Sid Jakes whistled softly through his teeth. "That's a neat trick. After all this time, what have they come up with?"

Metaxa looked over at him. "We don't know. Practically nothing is known about the world. They have never encouraged visitors from elsewhere, and certainly not United Planets."

Ronny was frowning. "But earlier you said that they've applied for membership."

"Yes, and that's what we're wondering about. Why? For a long time, since Einstein was first colonized, they've held themselves aloof. Absolutely haughty. A too-good-for-us sort of attitude. The only communication they usually have is with the most technologically advanced planets, such as Avalon. From time to time they'll send delegations to such worlds and swap scientific knowledge, and technological know-how. Usually, from what our records show, they have more to give than to receive, but from time to time they pick up something that they, themselves, have thus far not hit upon."

Dorn Horsten said slowly, "It would seem to me that the acquisition of such a world as Einstein would fit in with the basic purpose of Section G. That is, to upgrade the human race, scientifically, technologically, so that when and if we come up against alien intelligent life we'll be most suited to deal with it, on either friendly or other basis."

"That is what we are hoping for," Metaxa said. "But we still wonder at their motivation, at this late date. What if we bring them into our confederation, a world that is intellectually superior to such an extent that they might be able to take over, lock, stock and barrel, our institutions?" He shrugged and let his moist eyes go from Horsten to Ronny Bronston. "At any rate, that's your assignment. To go to Einstein and thoroughly case the planet."

Ronny said, "What's our cover?"

"You have none. You don't need any. You are preliminary representatives sent by the Commissariat of Interplanetary Affairs to investigate the workings of a world that has applied for membership. Nothing could be more reasonable. Later, after your report, if they are found acceptable, then, undoubtedly, a delegation from United Planets, probably including the President himself, will come to welcome them to membership."

He wrapped it up. "You play it straight. You should have no difficulty whatsoever. As I said earlier, it should be like a vacation."

Ronny's face held puzzlement. "It doesn't sound like my type of assignment. Why me? And why Dorn, for that matter? We're both trouble shooters, hatchet men, as someone unkindly put it once."

Metaxa sighed and eyed his bottle for a moment, but then shook his head and picked it up and returned it reluctantly to the drawer. He said, "Because we put it on the computers and out of all the thousands of Probationary Agents, First Grade Agents, Supervisor Agents, and all others, Doctor Horsten had the highest intelligence rating and you had second highest. Your experience, of course, is greater than Horsten's, so the two of you go to this damned brain world."

Ronny Bronston was flabbergasted. He had never thought of himself as having more than average intelligence.

Metaxa said sourly, "But, even so, don't play any battle chess with them. We can't afford to show ourselves up."

Doctor Horsten said mildly, "They don't play battle chess. The chap I met on Firenze introduced me to their planetary intellectual game. I couldn't make heads nor tails of the rules and gave up. It was too advanced for me. Evidently, on Einstein, even the children play it."

Sid Jakes, characteristically, was chuckling. He said to Metaxa, "When they put into the computers the request for who had the highest intelligence in Section G, Chief, how did you rate?"

The Commissioner glared at him. "Shut up, you laughing hyena," he growled. "You don't need brains to get places in Section G. You're the classic example."

"I resemble that remark," Sid Jakes said with mock dignity.

Metaxa said to Ronny and Dorn Horsten, "There it is. The sooner you get going, the better. The

Director of the Commissariat isn't too happy about this. I had to talk him into it. To him, it smacks of insincerity on our part. We should welcome them with open arms to our confideration of planets."

Dorn Horsten had been straightening out the barrel of his Section G H-gun.

Sid Jakes laughed and said, "Forget about it. We'll issue you another one. You'd never be able to hit a building with that shooter, after what you did to the barrel."

"I hate guns," Horsten said.

Metaxa said, "That reminds me. You two will take your communicators but not your H-guns, nor any other Section G equipment, no matter how hideable. They'd probably have metal detectors and so forth at the spaceport and it would look suspicious for you to arrive on your type of mission armed. Einstein is said to be one of the richest, one of the most scientifically advanced, planets settled by man. They undoubtedly have all sorts of ways to detect anything off-beat about you two."

"Got it," Ronny said, coming to his feet. "How do we get there? Do we have a Space Forces craft assigned to us?"

His superior shook his head. "No. You play it very unostentatiously. You travel by commercial carrier. First class, but not in one of the most expensive staterooms. On Einstein, if you are not offered accommodations by the authorities, you stay in a good hotel, but not a deluxe one. You play everything very earnest, very sincere."

5

They had a several-day wait before getting a
spacecraft going through to Einstein, and spent it
getting their stories straight. They were both to be
from the Commissariat of Interplanetary Affairs,
but not from the Bureau of Investigation and
certainly not from Section G. Irene Kasansky had
new papers done up for them. Metaza had the
Director of the Commissariat write letters of
introduction. Dorn Horsten's wardrobe was already
properly conservative for a plenipotentiary but
Ronny Bronston ordered a complete new outfit.

They were even interviewed by a newsman.

Sid Jakes made arrangements for them to be
assigned an office in the main section of the
Commissariat so that the reporter wouldn't smell a
rat. There must be no indication that Section G was
in any manner connected with the mission.

Properly seated and with a drink on the small
table next to his chair, the reporter said, "I'm Nick
Pond. Now, let's see. You're Doctor Dorn M.
Horsten, eminent biologist, originally from the
member planet Brobdingnag."

"That is correct," Dorn nodded politely.

The reporter turned to Ronny. "And you are
Citizen Ronald Bronston, born here on Earth, and
formerly employed by Population Statistics in New
Copenhagen, but now a diplomat for the Commiss-

ariat of Interplanetary Affairs."

Ronny pursed his lips judiciously. "Diplomat is possibily not quite the word, Citizen Pond. Doctor Horsten and I are merely an advance party going to Einstein to make the preliminary arrangements for that world to join the United Planets."

"*What* preliminary arrangements? I've never heard of such a mission before."

Ronny nodded agreement. "You are quite correct. This is the first time it has ever been done. You see, although Einstein was one of the very early planets to be colonized by mankind, we know very little about it. We are to report upon their institutions such as their government, their socio-economic system, their..."

"Just a minute," Nick Pond said. "Wouldn't that be interfering with their internal affairs, as prohibited by Articles One and Two of the United Planets Charter?"

"Of course not," Ronny said. "The Charter applies only to members of the United Planets. Einstein is not as yet a member."

The reporter scowled but looked at Dorn Horsten and said, "I looked up your career in our news morgue as an algae research specialist. Why would a biologist be sent on an expedition such as this?"

The doctor pushed his pince-nez glasses back further on the bridge of his nose and beamed at him. He said, "Einstein is known to be one of the most scientifically oriented worlds in the known galaxy. Surely, it is appropriate that a scientist be sent in to the preliminary negotiations. I look forward to making new friends, finding new colleagues."

Nick Pond frowned and looked off into unseen

distances. He muttered, "Something doesn't ring true about this. It's never been done before."

Ronny stiffened. All this damned newshawk had to do was broadcast his suspicions and just as sure as the Holy Ultimate made little green apples it would get back to Einstein, and they'd be on their guard.

He said, "Citizen Pond, could I make some off the record comments?"

The other eyed him. "Wizard."

"All right. It's true that this is a new departure. And it's time for it, too. There are now 2436 worlds that belong to our confederation. When United Planets was first conceived of and organized, it was even looser than it is now. We let in anybody without the slightest investigation whatsoever. And some of them were truly far-out. However, once in, there was no provision in the United Planets Charter for expelling a world that was a member, unless it violated Article Two. As a result, we allowed to join such planets as Stalin, whose socio-economic system was an early and vicious form of communism. On the other extreme was Phrygia, governed by an ambitious dictator and militarist. And New Delos, a theocracy, ruled by a supposed immortal God-King, who ground down the people unmercifully. Happily, the government was overthrown on Stalin and New Delos too, for that matter, after the God-King was assassinated by his subjects. And Phrygia was destroyed in a catastrophe still unexplained."

The reporter said, "Your point being that United Planets wishes to be more selective in the future?"

"Yes. At the time she was destroyed, Phrygia, which was militarily far advanced, was making plans to dominate first her closer neighbors, then all of

United Planets. We want no more such members in our ranks."

"I see. But why Einstein? I understand, though we have practically nothing on her in our data banks, she's composed of a citizenry of, ah, stutes, ah, eggheads they called them in the old days."

"No particular reason for Einstein. You have to start somewhere. As you say, we know very little about her. That is why Doctor Horsten and I are going to make a preliminary investigation."

Ronny smiled wryly. "For all we know, perhaps all of these brains have gone to their head."

The reporter laughed dutifully and came to his feet. "Well, thanks, gentlemen. And have a good trip. I'll mention it in passing on my program but won't play it up."

They stood, too, and went through the standard amenities.

Pond smiled and said, "I won't mention the fact that you're really a couple of snoops for United Planets."

The following day they took the shuttle from Greater Washington to Neuve Albuquerque and booked passage on the passenger-freighter SF *Sheppard*.

It was a strictly routine interplanetary journey and both Ronny and Dorn Horsten had been on a dozen or more spacecraft similar to the *Sheppard*. Routine was the only word. Somehow, the faster man travels, the less interesting the trip becomes. If one walks, one experiences much, sees a good deal. There is less if one rides a horse, or bicycles. There is still less if one speeds along a road in an automobile, and still less when the road becomes a superhighway and speed can be doubled. Still less does one experience in an airliner; aside from take-off and landing, there is precious little to do or see. But space travel, especially in under-space? Pure boredom.

All passengers—there were only three besides Dorn Horsten and Ronny—ate at the captain's table.

At the first dinner in space, the skipper fixed his eyes on the two Section G agents. He was a grumpy old spacehound and should have been beyond retirement age. However, some of the planets specializing in interplanetary commerce, and often using over-aged space freighters, sometimes hired these old timers, since they could get them more cheaply. The aged spacehounds, after a lifetime going about the galaxy, found it impossible to adjust to surface life, and hung onto any job they could get that would keep them in interplanetary travel.

He said, "So you're going to Einstein?"

Ronny sensed an opportunity to learn something additional about their destination. He said, "Why, yes. You've been there before?"

"Often," the captain growled, breaking a roll in disgust. "It's part of our regular run. Worst liberty set-down in the system. The crew hate it. I don't blame them. Seldom leave my ship, myself, but spacemen need relaxation between jumps."

Dorn and Ronny both looked at him questioningly.

The doctor said casually, in his mild voice, "What's wrong with Einstein?"

"Nothing."

They still looked at him.

He buttered his roll. The other passengers, three

men, all of whom were obviously in interplanetary commerce, didn't bother to listen. The ennui of space had already set in.

He said, "And nothing right, either, from a spaceman's viewpoint. There's nothing to do."

Ronny said, "How do you mean?"

"There's not even a bar at the spaceport. You can't understand the Tri-Di. Even if you could, the kind of shows they run you can't..."

Ronny said, "What do you mean, you can't understand the Tri-Di?"

"They don't speak Basic, or even Amer-English."

"Oh. You mean on none of the programs? I've been on planets, such as Paris, where they continue to speak an old Earth language called French, or that damned Neu Reich, where they speak German, but everybody spoke Basic as well, and a good many of the theatres and Tri-Di and TV shows were in it, usually entertainment they'd imported from other planets."

"On none of the programs," the captain growled. "The cloddies never import entertainment from other planets. They make it clear they think it's too juvenile."

Ronny took a sip of wine before saying, still in puzzlement, "But there must be other types of entertainment in the cities besides those dependent on language—nightclubs, bars..."

"There are no cities. Even if there were, there wouldn't be any nightclubs or bars. From what I hear, they don't drink alcohol, or anything else that's supposedly bad for your health, for that matter. Not even coffee."

Dorn Horsten said, "No cities?"

"They don't like them."

Ronny said in protest, "But you've got to have cities."

"Evidently, they don't think so," the captain said. "I was talking to one of their customs officials, if that's what you could call him, once, and he explained it to me. He said that, by the time the colonists arrived on Einstein from Earth, cities were already what he called an anachronism. The original reasons for being no longer applied. Originally, they were centers for defense, centers for trade, centers for manufacture, education, religion. Obviously, the defense reason is out now. In modern warfare, where you still find it at all, a city is just a sitting duck. And with modern methods of transportation, computers and automation, you can put your manufacturing plants and distribution centers anywhere. You don't need a city for them. And with modern communications and planet-wide data banks, you don't need cities for educational centers. As far as religion is concerned, damn few people are religious any more, especially on Einstein, but you can always tune in Tri-Di if you want to hear a sermon."

"Well, this is a new one for me," Ronny said. "I've never been on a planet that didn't have at least small cities. Don't they even have towns?"

"No. They like privacy and they don't like congestion, pollution and the other alleged shortcomings of cities and towns."

One of the other passengers, a red-faced type, yawned and said, "Have you all heard the one about the lovelorn gorilla? It's the funniest dirty joke I ever heard."

6

Einstein began its peculiarity right from the beginning.

The skipper himself saw them to the gangplank, followed by two spacemen with their luggage. He had amusement in his gruff expression. It was a small spaceport with only two other craft on it. Both of them looked like interplanetary tramps. It would seem that Einstein wasn't exactly much of a center of traffic.

Ronny and Dorn looked out over the pavement upon which the *Sheppard* had just landed. Three automated stevedore carts were hustling toward them; otherwise, the whole area was empty, save for a natty hover car parked only a few meters away. The sole occupant was a girl.

There were no buildings lining the field. Where the metallic-looking landing area ended, there was what looked like nothing so much as an Earth-side golf course. A bit more rolling, perhaps, than a golf course, including ponds and small lakes, and clumps of trees. In general, the first impression was than Einstein was earthlike to within a few percentage points. Either that, or the planetary engineers had gone to great effort to make it so.

Ronny took in the captain, who was grinning deprecation. Ronny said, "Where in the hell are the administration buildings, the freight terminals, the spaceport hotel and so on?"

The captain said, "Damned if I know."

Ronny looked at him and said, "Thanks. But you warned us. This must be a helluva liberty set-down for your boys."

"Not even a place to get a beer," the captain told him. He'd obviously accompanied them for the sole purpose of witnessing their astonishment. He said, "I suppose that mopsy down there is your welcoming committee."

"Welcoming committee?" Dorn Horsten said blankly. "We're a delegation from the Commissariat of Interplanetary Affairs, from United Planets. The first that's ever come from Earth. I was, ah, rather expecting a band or so, blaring the planetary anthem of Einstein and possibly that of United Planets. A welcoming committee of a dozen or so elderly looking types with red sashes across their chests. Possibly a company or so of soldiers to be reviewed."

"You dreamer," the captain laughed sourly. "Have fun, gents."

Ronny and Horsten started down the gangplank, followed by the two spacemen with their bags.

They approached the hover car, and, as they did, the girl came out of it, smiling.

On her, a smile was something. She was a very blonde, in the Scandinavian tradition. No, in the Finnish tradition, which is the blondest of the Scandinavians. Her hair was impossibly fine and light yellow almost to the point of being white. Her eyes were so blue as to be startling. Her features reminded Ronny Bronston of an actress of yester-year that he had seen several times in historical movie films—Jean Simmons. Her lips were implausibly red, but, very obviously, not due to cosmetics.

She was dressed in a gorgeous brilliantly-white blouse and a kilt that resembled those of Crete in the days of Knossos and King Minos. Her slippers were in the Etruscan revival style, which Ronny had last seen on the planet Shangri-La. Her figure was the unfulfilled dream of a Tri-Di director of sex shows.

"Holy smokes," Ronny said under his breath as they approached her.

"Indeed, yes," Dorn murmured back. "I find that I'm not nearly as old as I thought I was."

She spoke to them brightly and her voice, though perhaps a trifle sultry, matched her physical appearance. It reached down inside you and grabbed. She said, "I am Rosemary. Welcome to Einstein. You are, of course, the celebrated Doctor Dorn M. Horsten and..." she smiled at Ronny in a blaze "...Ronald Bronston."

Ronny said, in mock protest, even as they shook hands, Earth fashion, "I'm celebrated too. Sometimes with fireworks."

"Yes," she said, still smiling. "So we are aware. I should have said, the *notorious* Ronny Bronston."

Oh, oh. He had been trying to jest. But, on the face of it, the powers that be on Einstein knew he was the trouble shooter extraordinary of Section G. That wasn't so good. But at least he knew that they knew.

Rosemary said, "I am your guide. I am completely at your service."

Dorn said gallantly, "Do your authorities always send such charming guides?"

She smiled at him, and there was a pixie quality there that seemed out of place in her classical beauty. "As a biologist, Doctor Horsten, you will be interested in knowing that on Einstein we breed for

60

physical attributes as well as mental ones."

So, Ronny thought inwardly, she is perfectly aware of how exceptionally attractive she is. He was to find out later that she wasn't; only average for Einstein.

He said, "We weren't expected?"

She made motions for the spacemen to place the luggage in the hover car. They had been staring at her as though hypnotized. The look in their eyes was such as to be almost an unsult. Only a spark would be needed for them to throw her to the tarmac and attempt rape. They sighed resignation and male frustration and did their duty and left.

She politely gestured to seats in the vehicle as she said, "Oh yes, of course. We received the space cable from the Octagon that you were to arrive. Why in the name of the Holy Ultimate do they call it a space cable? On the face of it, cables are not exactly practical in interplanetary communications."

"A left over expression from the past," Dorn Horsten said mildly. "But aren't there any of your officials..." He let the sentence dribble away.

"We don't have officials on Einstein," she said, activating the car.

Ronny closed his eyes in pain at that one.

She said, heading at a good clip for the nearest area of the golf course, "Would you prefer speaking in Basic rather than Amer-English?"

"Either will do, my dear," Dorn Horsten told her. "See here, how do you mean there are no officials? We came to initiate negotiations in view of your request to join United Planets. With whom do we deal?"

"A committee has been elected to meet you

61

personally, Doctor Horsten."

Ronny said, "Wizard. Uh, where's the committee and how do you mean personally? How else could they meet us?"

She tinkled a laugh that all but had the Section G agents swooning. "We very seldom conduct affairs personally, Citizen Bronston. The time involved in journeying about for such reasons is ridiculous. We perform business and even most of our personal relationships by Tri-Di phone screen. Certainly this applies on such advanced planets as Earth, and, say, Phrygia and Avalon."

"Phrygia we no longer have with us," Ronny told her. "But yes, a good deal of business is transacted by TV phone these days. Why travel half way around the world to make a short-time contact?"

"Certainly," she said winningly. "But the committee is to meet you in person tomorrow. They will journey from their respective homes."

Ronny assimilated that. He said, not knowing exactly why, "All right. But why were you—I have no objections, of course—chosen to meet us?"

"Because I'm stupid," she said brightly, flashing an equally bright smile at him.

They had reached the edge of the pavement and were darting over the fabulous lawn and rolling grounds of the area that surrounded it. Suddenly they were confronted by an entry into a hillside that formerly hadn't been visible. She entered without slowing and sighed and flicked off a switch.

"I dislike driving manually," she said.

They were in an underground highway. There wasn't a great deal of other traffic. The other vehicles they did see were sometimes occupied, more often

62

not. It wasn't as different as all that. Ronny and Dorn had been on other worlds, including Earth, that had highly automated underground highways. However, none of them were superior to this.

Ronny said carefully, "How do you mean, stupid? You're unhappy about taking the assignment?"

She looked at him in distress. "Oh, no, no. I applied for it. It's quite the most fascinating, uh, job, I've ever been able to land. I meant it literally. I'm stupid."

Horsten caught on first. The big doctor said, "You mean...you were chosen to communicate with us because you have a, forgive me, low intelligence?"

"Yes," she said. "Now in a few minutes we'll arrive at the quarters where you are to stay."

She looked at Doctor Horsten. "Don't misunderstand. I'm not an idiot. I'm just slow. As you said, forgive me, but they thought communication would be easier."

It was Dorn Horsten this time who closed his eyes in sorrow. In his time...well...in his time he had been accepted...well...in his time...

They emerged from the underground highway and again were in what seemed to be an overgrown park.

Rosemary took over the controls and said, "Why does everybody want to be smart?"

Ronny looked at her. "I don't know. Why?"

"It wasn't a rhetorical question. I meant it. I can see in primitive times, when it was a matter of survival and so forth, that a person had to be either smarter than the next, or stronger. But who cares about those things now? Look at Doctor Horsten.

He's big and, I assume, strong. But who cares if anybody is big or small any more? These are no longer the days of the Vikings. Why should anybody wish to be any larger than, say, a Japanese?"

"Damned if I know," Dorn Horsten muttered. "Often, it's a disadvantage. Half the beds that I try to get into in hotels are too small for me."

The vehicle rounded a hill and suddenly there was an entry. It was artfully framed in bougainvillaea of two different colors. It should have looked garish, but didn't. It was gorgeous. The entry was only a few meters deep and they emerged into a patio, open to the sky, graced by a fountain in its center.

"Here we are," Rosemary said cheerfully.

The two visitors looked up and about. There were various doors and windows built into what they had taken from outside to be a hill covered with grass, bushes and small trees.

"It's an underground house!" Ronny blurted.

"Yes, of course," she said, beginning to leave the vehicle.

Ronny sat there for a moment. He said, "Back there at the spaceport. All of the administration buildings, freight depots, that sort of thing, were also underground?"

"Yes, that's right. Few buildings are really attractive, especially those dealing with necessary production, distribution, communications and so on. So we place them out of sight where they won't interfere with nature's beauties. There are other advantages as well. They are easier to heat in the winter, or cool in summer."

The two men got out and looked about them for a moment. The patio was beautifully done, almost tropically lush with flowers and ferns.

Doctor Horsten said in appreciation, "Your gardener is to be congratulated."

"Gardener? I have no gardener. Can you gentlemen bring your bags?"

She led the way to two adjoining rooms, saying, "All rooms lead out on the garden. This will be yours, Doctor, and this yours, Citizen Bronston. Over here is the living room. I'll await you there."

Ronny entered his room, which amounted to a small suite; a bedroom, a bath, a small sitting room. It was very finely done but obviously with comfort in mind, not luxury. The furniture was functional, rather than pretty. He appreciated the single painting on the wall. It was in the Chinese tradition. The only other decorative bit was a vase which was either a Mexican pre-Columbian antique or a very good copy. Simplicity was highly regarded on Einstein, he decided. Or, at least, it was in this house.

He left his two bags and went out into the patio again, just as Dorn Horsten emerged from his own suite. They headed for the living room.

Rosemary was sitting on a sofa which faced on a very large window; so large, indeed, that it covered almost a full wall. Ronny, orienting himself, realized that it must be on the opposite side of the hill from where they had entered. There was a spectacular vista beyond. Most certainly they hadn't seen the window as they approached. This room carried out the theme of the suites—simple and ultracomfortable. Art was held to a minimum, but what there was, was superlative.

Rosemary came to her feet, smiling. She said, "Your quarters are adequate?"

"Charming," the doctor told her, bowing slightly in thanks.

"Wizard," Ronny said. "I'd like to steal that Chinese painting of the fog-bound mountain."

"It's yours," she said.

"Oh, really, I didn't mean..."

"But, of course. I'm so pleased that you appreicate a product of my humble efforts. And now, would you gentlemen like a drink?"

"Your humble efforts?" Ronny said, staring at her. "Do you mean you did that? I thought it came from Earth, or, at least, one of the Chinese-settled planets."

"Oh, no. All of us here on Einstein participate in at least one of the arts. Could I offer a light wine, or perhaps beer? It's warm today."

Dorn Horsten cleared his throat and said, "See here, my dear. How do you mean, all of you participate in at least one of the arts? Suppose someone has no talent. Is he *forced*, despite that, to participate in one of the arts?"

She laughed, as though in deprecation. "We are not happy about that term *talent*. We find that everyone has some inclination in the arts. Much of our raising of the young is devoted to discovering which one—we include, obviously, the handicrafts. From earliest youth, a child is carefully observed to find its particular tendencies and is encouraged to develop them. I had crayons and watercolors available to me from a period before I can actually remember. As I grew older there were teachers, some of them quite exceptional, to continue to channel my desire to draw and paint. Talent, usually, is the ability to work hard and long at one's chosen art.

What is the old saying? A lazy genius isn't one."

Ronny said, "About that drink. I was told you didn't drink alcohol on Einstein. Or even coffee, for that matter, on the grounds that it's bad for the health."

She went over to a beautifully worked piece of wooden furniture and opened two of its doors to emerge with glasses and a long, thin, green bottle, obviously chill. "Nonsense," she said. "Alcohol is a blessing come down from man's early days. I believe I read somewhere that there was only one race, in primitive times, that didn't work out some alcoholic beverage. They were, I believe, the Tasmanians and they contributed absolutely nothing to man's culture in any field. We don't utilize the distilled beverages but we enjoy the fermented and brewed. This is a local wine based on the Reisling grape which our people brought with them when they first emigrated from Earth."

She poured deftly into faintly green goblets and served them both before taking up her own glass.

She said, "To the entry of Einstein into the United Planets confederation."

They drank to the toast politely.

"Won't you be seated?" she said. "I'm sure that you have a good many questions."

Ronny said, seating himself, "Yes, your planet is quite unique."

She frowned slightly in puzzlement and said, "It is? I have never been over-space. In what way?"

He looked about him. "Well, this house for instance. It almost amounts to being a cave."

She tinkled a laugh again. "What's unique about that? A most practical manner in which to live.

Houses built on the surface almost invariably deface the landscape. They are ugly, especially when congested." She pointed upward. "Above us are grass, flowers, trees. Birds and animals find their homes in them. The plant life also releases oxygen into our atmosphere. If such was my hobby, I could even raise vegetables or fruit on my *roof*."

Ronny said, "When we were driving from the spaceport, did we pass other houses such as this?"

"Certainly. Quite a few."

"And they're all built so that one doesn't know he's passing a house unless he knows it's there?"

"Yes. We make almost a fetish of that." She took a breath—beautifully—and said, "But I'm being a terrible hostess. I get so caught up in talking to people who have actually come from other worlds. You must be famished."

In truth, the two had not eaten their mid-day meal, in anticipation of the landing of the *Sheppard* and the beginning of their new assignment.

Rosemary led the way to the dining room.

7

Dorn Horsten looked around appreciatively, as they seated themselves at the heavy table. He said, "This is your home? Ah, personally, I mean?"

She smiled at him. "Why, yes. As long as I wish to live in it."

"You said that you had no gardener. But otherwise you must require quite a staff."

"Staff?"

"Servants."

"Oh. There are no servants on Einstein."

Ronny eyed her in disbelief. "You mean that you do all the housework, including the gardening?"

She said, "Why, yes. The house is all but completely automated, you know. All houses are. Drudgery has been eliminated. Now, what will you gentlemen have?"

The table was obviously automated, but there was no menu set into its top, nor screen where a menu could be dialed.

Ronny cleared his throat and said, "What do you have? That is, uh, what are you pushing?"

The girl said, as though in surprise, "Why, anything."

The two Section G agents looked at her.

"Just anything at all, my dear?" Horsten said.

"Why, yes."

They blinked at her and Ronny said, "Now, look.

Peking Duck. Suppose I wanted Peking Duck as prepared on the planet Mandarin."

She said, projecting her voice out over the table, "An order of Peking Duck as prepared on the planet Mandarin," and then she looked questioningly at Doctor Horsten.

He looked back at her levelly and said, deliberately, "I'll have *antipasti cassalinghi*, *cannelloni*, both in the style of the planet Naples. Then *scallopine di vitello alla bolognese*, in the manner prepared on Firenze. All this with a bottle of Valpolicella."

"My, you *are* hungry," she said brightly, and repeated the order out over the table. "I am afraid that it won't be true Valpolicella but so nearly that it is unlikely that you'll tell the difference. The vintners among us, conscious of wine-making as an art, make a hobby of duplicating practically every vintage known."

Ronny said in exasperation, "Wait a minute. Do you mean to tell me you have automated kitchens that contain every known recipe on any Earthling settled world?"

That seemed to puzzzle her. "Don't you on Earth?"

Ronny said, "Possibly every cookbook ever published can be found in the United Planets Interplanetary Data Banks on Earth. But they're most certainly not hooked up to every automated kitchen in the world."

"Why not?"

The two men both blinked again.

"It would seem to be quite a project," Horsten demurred. "Besides, some of the raw materials wouldn't be available on Earth."

She sighed. "Yes, that *can* be a problem. When it

70

arises our chefs must improvise. I have a friend who has been working for years on duplicating Menelaus white fish, certainly one of the most delicate sea foods found in the galaxy."

She spoke again out over the table, this time in a language neither of her guests understood. Then she leaned back into her chair.

She said, "On Einstein, we consider cuisine to be one of the gentler arts, and make every effort to develop it. We, too, have every cook book ever published, in our data banks." She smiled mischeivously. "We secured most of them, indirectly, from your Earth-side data banks. Some time ago, we made a trade with the planet Catalina, technological information, developed here on Einstein, for the complete United Planets Data Banks. Of course, we have also developed recipes of our own."

Dorn Horsten was fascinated. He said, "Suppose I invented a new dish. How would I go about getting it into the automated restaurants' recipe banks? Who would decide?"

She frowned, again puzzled, and said, "No one. You'd just put it in, it would be crossfiled, and anybody who wanted to try it could."

Ronny said, grimly, "Suppose it was chocolate covered dill pickles with anchovy sauce."

She laughed at him. "Then I doubt if anybody would ever order it."

The table top sank down to return in moments with their dishes. She had evidently ordered largely salad for herself. Ronny's Peking Duck came garnished with various other Chinese dishes. He wished that he had ordered some hot sake, while he was at it.

Dorn looked down in despair at the great pile of

71

food he had summoned, but set to. He said, "To get back to that servants thing. You said there were none on Einstein. How about the wealthy?"

"What wealthy?"

He took her in, before saying, "I can see where people of ordinary means would utilize your high rate of automation to free themselves of the drudgery of housekeeping and the preparation of meals. But those with larger estates. Don't they maintain staffs of servants?"

"Oh," she said, frowning lightly as though wondering how to put this. "But, you see, there are no wealthy on Einstein. When our people first came here it must have been one of the best funded colonizations that Earthlings have ever embarked upon. They quickly built the most modern automated and computerized industries, the most efficient possible and ever since we've been upgrading it. There are no poor and no wealthy on Einstein. There is absolute abundance for everyone."

"Utopia!" Ronny blurted, in disbelief.

She shook her head and her frown deepened. She said, "No, certainly not. There is no such thing as Utopia. It means perfection, which is a goal that can never be achieved. As you approach, it recedes, and you have new achievements to strive toward."

Her eyes went back to Dorn Horsten. "We have no *personal* servants, but, often, an outstanding scientist may have assistants, or an outstanding artist might have one or more apprentices. An outstanding writer might have someone to help him with his research. But none of these are really servants."

Dinner over, Rosemary murmured something out

72

over the table in her unknown language and the table center sank in, taking the soiled dishes away.

They headed back for the living room.

Dorn Horsten said, "What is that language you speak? I don't believe I've ever heard it before."

"I would imagine not, Doctor. I doubt if it is spoken anywhere except on Einstein. It's a scientific language, largely a combination of Esperanto and Interlingua, though our own experts made deletions, or additions, of their own."

Ronny said, "Look, let's put this on a more informal basis. I can't keep calling you nothing but Rosemary, while you call me Citizen Bronston, and Dorn, Doctor Horsten. What *is* your last name, by the way?"

"I have none. My name's just Rosemary."

Again the two men looked at her blankly.

Ronny said, "I meant your family name."

"Yes, I know. But I have no family. My name's Rosemary and my identification number is F-123-B-1495. That, of course, is for the data banks."

"But you've got to have a family. Do you mean that you are an orphan?"

"There are no, well, orphans, on Einstein. Either that, or I suppose that you could say we're all orphans. But there are no families."

Ronny said plaintively, "You've got to have families. There's always been the family."

"No there hasn't," she told him. "Certainly not in the sense in which you're speaking. I would imagine that for ninety percent of the history of the human race, the pairing family, such as you still know it on Earth and elsewhere in United Planets, was unknown. That is a man, a woman and their children, the children taking the man's name upon birth. The extended family applied for most of man's history.

Dorn Horsten said gently, "We seem to have drifted away from the fascinating point. You said that you have no families on Einstein any longer."

Rosemary turned her impossibly blue eyes to him. "There's no need for them. Property is no longer an issue. There is none. Parents are no longer involved in having their possessions descend to their off-spring."

"Now, wait a minute," Ronny said. "I've been losing things all along in this conversation, that really took a wheel off however. What do you mean, there is no property? You were telling us a little while ago that everybody had it made on Einstein. That there was an abundance for everybody."

"Of course," she told him, nodding her head. "But there is no private property."

Dorn Horsten said, thinking he got it, "You mean that you have established communism on Einstein?"

She sent her eyes over to the doctor and frowned her absolutely beautiful frown at him. "It's an elastic term... Dorn," she said. "If you mean the so-called communism first established by Lenin on Earth, and later extended to such planets as Stalin, then no."

Ronny said, his voice irritated and demanding. "Then what do you mean no private ownership? You told us earlier that this was your house."

"You misunderstood," she told him. "It is mine in the sense that I occupy it. But it isn't *mine*. Or anybody else's. Who in the name of the Holy Ultimate would want to be tied down to a house?" She stated it as though that was the most reasonable

74

position possible. But then she added, "Of course I *own*, I suppose you could say, my *personal* things; my toothbrush, my art objects, my favorite articles of clothing—the ones I don't send down the disposal chutes every day. So does everybody else."

Ronny closed his eyes momentarily. "To get back to this 'no family' thing. Suppose a man and woman want to live together?"

"Then they do, for as long as both want to. Any number of men and women who wish to live together can."

"Wizard," Ronny said triumphantly. "And suppose that they have a baby?"

"If the genetics computers okay it, they do."

Ronny looked at her, but then shook his head. "We'll get back to that later. You've got a man, a woman and a child. Isn't that a family?"

"No. Any one of the three can leave at any time." She added, "Children are no longer dependent on their parents."

"You mean the state raises all children?"

"There is no state on Einstein. Children are the responsibility of society."

"Then a couple of parents aren't allowed to raise their own child?" Dorn said.

"Certainly they are, if the computers find that they are competent to do so. However, few people desire to. Children have always been a drag. In the past you were taught that it was your duty to raise your offspring, no matter how incompetent you might be to do so. You also supposedly loved them, whatever that means. Your early education in your home, your schools, your religious institutions, all taught that you must love and raise your children. It is no longer necessary to raise them, and we are somewhat sceptical about the meaning of love. It's too elastic a term to make much sense."

"Confound it," Ronny said. "Who raises the kid?"

"People who are competent to do so, and who are particularly fond of children. There are always ample volunteers to go into that field of endeavor." She came to her feet and said, "But I'm being a terrible hostess again. Dorn, I note that you have a taste for Italian food. Would you like a glass of Marsala as a nightcap? I can recommend it. And you, Ronald?"

They both accepted and she went off for it.

Ronny said to Dorn, "I've still got a good many questions, obviously, but it still sounds like a Utopia to me. Why in the hell do they want to join United Planets? What have we got to offer them?"

"That's what we're here to find out," Dorn Horsten said, his voice also low. "Don't have to raise your children, eh? Sounds like a Utopia at that. I never have liked children. One of the reasons I've never gotten married. We have some rather prudish institutions on the planet of my birth."

Rosemary returned with three glasses and a dark bottle and served them.

She smiled brightly and said, "Now then, where were we? We seem to go off on tangents. Before I can answer one of your questions, two more have popped up."

Ronny said, "Rosemary, you mentioned the genetics computers, and later you mentioned that two people could raise their own child if the computers decided they were competent. Suppose the computers decided against them in one or the other case, or both. And suppose they wanted the child anyway and wanted to raise it, and the hell with the computers."

Rosemary finished her wine and put down her glass before answering. She said, very seriously, "Genetics are our strongest *raison d-être*. It is the reason Einstein was colonized. Anyone refusing to conform to our institutions pertaining to genetics is perfectly free to leave Einstein and seek what he desires on some other planet."

She looked at her watch. "But you two must be tired. And you're to have a full day tomorrow. Is bed in order?"

The two men stood. "I suppose that you're right, my dear," the doctor said. "And perhaps we should mull over some of the things that you have already told us. It's all been fascinating."

She stood too and smiled her dazzling bright smile and said, "Would either, or both of you, like me to sleep with you?"

8

Dorn Horsten had always been a light sleeper, and since he had affiliated himself with Section G and the United Planets dream had become even more so. The cloak and dagger assignments he had been given had a tendency to sharpen the senses. A stirring brought him instantly awake.

When Rosemary had made her startling offer, obviously thinking nothing of it, both of the Section G agents had boggled at her. If she had suddenly grown an elephant's trunk, they could hardly have been more surprised.

But Doctor Horsten had no taste for group sex, and he had noticed all evening that Ronny could hardly keep his eyes off the pretty girl. So, as politely as possible under the circumstances, the doctor had begged off, explaining that he was overtired and realized that the day ahead was to be a full one. He went off to bed, leaving Ronny and the beauteous Rosemary to their arrangements.

He had no idea, when he was awakened, what time it was or how long he had slept. Einstein had no moon, and hence nightlight was dependent upon the stars. True, the atmosphere was extremely clear, and the distant suns shone bright, but still there was little light coming through the large windows which opened onto the patio.

There was no lock on the door, allowing for easy

entry into his suite, and, in spite of the dimness, Dorn Horsten realized that someone had taken advantage of the fact. Indeed, there were two of them, and at first he couldn't make out what they were up to.

By their bulk, they were both men and, though not of Horsten's size, substantial nevertheless. As his eyes grew more accustomed to the room, he made out what seemed to be masks, or goggles, on their faces and both seemed to be carrying what he would have guessed were flashlights, though neither of them were lit. He wished he could take up his glasses from the night table, but that would only alert them.

They were bending over something on the floor, and at first he couldn't make out what the object was. Then it came to him. They were going through one of his suitcases. And to one side was the other one, open. It had obviously already been ransacked.

He was completely awake now.

Suddenly he threw back the covers and was on them, hoping fervently that the objects they carried weren't weapons. If they were some sort of laser or other advanced weapon developed on this planet, he'd undoubtedly had it.

The scrambling fight turned out to be a farce. There was insufficient light for anyone involved to operate with any sort of efficiency. All three of them, at one time or the other, were on the floor, or stumbling about, unable to make contact in the dark.

On top of that, Dorn Horsten was pulling his punches. He knew perfectly well that a full blow from his ham-sized fist would have caved in the rib cage of one of the intruders, and he was not on

Einstein to commit mayhem. He was here on peaceful mission, simply to gain information. From what Rosemary had said, the citizens of Einstein probably took a dim view of violence. The member worlds of United Planets which boasted the highest standards of living almost invariably had little criminal activity. Crime, except crimes of passion, deals almost exclusively with property, and when there is plenty for all, crime withers. And from what he learned thus far about Einstein, it had possbily the highest standard of living of any world Dorn had ever seen.

Suddenly the strangers disentangled themselves and were gone out the unlocked door.

His first inclination was to pursue, if for no other reason than to find out who they were. But he drew himself up before dashing out the door after them. For all he knew, those *were* weapons they carried and if they found themselves being followed, they might attempt to finish him. Besides, he knew nothing about the vicinity and the way these underground houses were camouflaged he wasn't sure that he'd be able to find his way back, if he got more than a few meters from the entry to Rosemary's home.

He waited a few minutes, to be sure they'd gotten well away, then went over and flicked on the lights. He picked up his glasses and anchored them firmly to his nose, then turned to inspect the damage.

The intruders hadn't been neat. The contents of his bags were strewn all over the floor.

So far as he could find, nothing was gone. For that matter, there was nothing that he could think of that might interest them. The Section G boys at headquarters had carefully selected the things that he and Ronny were to take to Einstein with them. No weapons, no secret gismos from the Department of Dirty Tricks. Nothing to make their hosts at all suspicious.

He was puzzled. It simply made no sense at all. If the locals had wanted to search his luggage, why hadn't they done it at the spaceport when he and Ronny had first emerged from the *Sheppard*? They hadn't even seen a customs man, an immigration officer, or any other authority. Of course, in a sense, Ronny Bronston and he came under the head of a mission, and diplomatic immunity could be said to apply to them, and hence their luggage woudln't have been inspected. But it was drawing rather a fine point to leave their things politely unexamined upon entry to the planet, and then sneak, at night, into a man's bedroom and search it. Still, he couldn't believe the two to be sneak thieves. From what Rosemary had said, there was no need on Einstein to be a thief. Certainly not a common pilferer.

He shrugged his heavy shoulders. It was a mystery.

Then his eyes fell upon something he had thus far missed. Up against the wall was one of the flashlight-like devices the others had carried. It had obviously been dropped in the confusion. He went over and picked it up, and, almost immediately, realized what it was. It was an infra-red flashlight. Those goggles they had worn were not masks, but were to enable them to utilize the light, which was useless to the naked eye.

They had come well prepared for their burglary.

He wondered, momentarily, whether or not he

should go next door to Ronny's room and inform him of what had happened but then shook his head. It could wait until morning. For one thing, he wasn't sure he wanted to tell about it in front of Rosemary. For another, he wasn't even sure Ronny was in his own suite; he might be in the girl's rooms. But even if he was in his own bed, he was probably busy at his masculine duties. And by the looks of Rosemary, those duties would continue far into the night.

He looked at the door for a moment and wondered if there wasn't some way to brace it. His eyes went about the small suite. The furniture didn't seem to be particularly suited. However, he took up one of the twin beds bodily and carried over to the door and braced it against the entry. At least, anyone trying to get back in would make enough noise to supply adequate warning. For all he knew, the two intruders might have second thoughts and decide to return, possibly with weapons this time, and finish him off. Dorn Horsten looked forward to dying in bed, some far day, but not from having been shot there.

9

Switching from the hours kept on the *Sheppard* to those of Einstein had thrown Ronny's sleeping schedule off, and he found himself awake at an earlier hour than he had expected. He looked over at Rosemary, whose blond head was on the pillow next to him. She was out like a light, and was even making a very small snore. Even after the wild night they had put in, and in the harsh light of morning, she still looked like the most beautiful woman he had ever bedded.

Moving very carefully, so as not to awaken her, he got up and carried one of his bags into the small sitting room, along with the clothes he had worn the day before. Possibly here on Einstein they disposed of clothing after one day's wear, but, even had he wanted to emulate them, he didn't know how to go about ordering new ones. Besides, he and Dorn hadn't met the committee Rosemary had mentioned and he decided to continue his ultra-conservative attire until they had. Ronny didn't particularly like it but he didn't particularly look the diplomatic type—though Dorn pulled it off very well—and conservative clothes would help.

They had both slept nude. He went into the bath and had little trouble figuring out the fixtures. He had figured out bathroom fixtures of many a culture in his time, including an outhouse on the anarchist planet Bakunin. This on Einstein was quite similar to those on Earth and the other advanced planets. He even found depilatory and used it on his beard.

His toilet over, he returned to the sitting room and, still as quietly as possible, to refrain from interrupting the slumber of his bedmate, dressed in fresh underthings, fresh socks and shirt, but otherwise in the same suit he had worn the day before.

He quietly let himself out onto the patio and from there went into the living room. He found Dorn Horsten in the dining room, having coffee and toast. Evidently, his sleep, too, had been upset by the change in schedule.

He smiled self-satisfaction and said, "I figured out how to order coffee on this table. I've never seen an automated table before that didn't at least have an order screen. In fact, I don't believe I've ever seen an automated table in a home out in the boondocks like this. However, I suppose that if you can pipe electricity, water and gas into a home from a distant point there's no particular reason why you couldn't send food from some automated kitchen. They probably have a vacuum tube arrangement."

"Coffee?" Ronny said, taking a seat across from the other. "I thought that coffee wasn't drunk on Einstein."

"That captain didn't know what he was talking about. He also said that they didn't drink alcohol. Whatever we find here on Einstein, it *won't* be an austere way of life. I'll wager he never got out of his space freighter here.

"Wizard. Order me a cup of coffee, some croissants and some orange marmalade."

Dorn Horsten projected his voice over the table and repeated the order.

While Ronny was waiting for it, his companion told him about the happenings of the night before.

Ronny stared at him. "What in the name of the Holy Ultimate were they looking for?"

"I can't come up with anything."

The light breakfast arrived and Ronny set to, scowling

He said, finally, "From what little we've seen and heard so far it doesn't seem to be a planet where you'd run into burglars. They dont even bother to put locks on the doors."

Dorn could only nod and poured more coffee for himself. "You'd think this was Earth-side coffee," he said, "or even better."

Ronny said, "And this marmalade obviously was made from real oranges. It's seldom you get good citrus fruit off Earth."

When he had finished his croissants, they took up fresh cups of coffee and went out into the living room.

After they were seated, Dorn said, "Did you find out anything special, after we separated last night?"

"Yeah," Ronny said. "They have sex tutors for the kids here. Give them a course in how to perform in bed, after they become adolescent."

Horsten snorted. "That'd make for a howl on Virtue. They still wear Mother Hubbards there."

"It'd make for a howl on some of the other backward worlds," Ronny said. "But not enough to keep Einstein out of United Planets. I still wonder why in the hell they want to bother to join. They've got it made. What can we do for them?"

A voice from the door said, "Am I intruding?"

The newcomer was accompanied by a male dog who had short and dark golden hair, and even golden eyes, and a bobbed tail, and who would possibly weigh seventy-five pounds. It was a beautiful hound. The man himself seemed to be approximately fifty years of age, was handsome and distinguished of face, looked very intelligent and wore kilts very similar to the ones Rosemary had on the day before. Somehow, on him they looked quite masculine, while on Rosemary they had not detracted from her femininity.

The two Section G agents put down their cups and came to their feet.

"Certainly not," Dorn Horsten said. "I am Doctor Dorn Horsten and this..."

"Is the famed Ronald Bronston," the other smiled, advancing. "My name is Fredric."

They shook hands, Earth-style.

Fredric said, "I am one of the committee elected to meet you. It is a pleasure. That coffee smells excellent. I think I shall go to Rosemary's dining room and get a cup."

Ronny and Dorn sat down again and took up their beverages.

Ronny said, "He doesn't sound any more of an egghead than anybody else."

The dog came over and extended his right paw and said to Ronny, "Hello, glad to meet you."

Ronny looked at him for a long empty moment, before shaking the paw.

The dog said, "What's your name again?"

"Ronny. What's yours?"

The golden dog hung his long red tongue out from

86

the side of his mouth and gave a double pant before saying, looking all the world as though he was embarrassed. "Boy. These people have no imagination. I suppose I shouldn't complain. I've got a friend they call Fido."

He turned and went over to Dorn Horsten, who was gaping at him as much as was Ronny. He held out his paw and said, "Glad to meet you, too."

Dorn shook and said, "The feeling is mutual. I am absolutely fascinated to meet you."

The dog sat down on the floor and looked up at him. "You're from Earth, aren't you? I understand that dogs don't talk on Earth. Why not?"

The eminent biologist looked at him blankly. "It never occurred to me to wonder about it," he said.

Fredric came back from the dining room, coffee cup in hand. He was smiling and had evidently heard the last of the conversation. He said to Boy, "On Earth, practically no animals, save man, have voice boxes. Some that do, such as the parrot, the Myna bird, and, to a certain extent, the higher anthropoid apes, have insufficient brain capacity to utilize them intelligently. Now, that will be all for the time, Boy."

"Okay," Boy said and stretched out on the floor.

"Now wait a minute," Dorn blurted. "This isn't a farce, is it? I mean, you're not a ventriloquist?"

"No. Certainly not," Fredric told him, after taking a sip of his coffee. "When our people left Earth for Einstein, we brought with us quite a bit of the fauna of the mother planet. Man's immediate pets, such as the dog and cat, who have come down with him through the millenia, almost as though there was a symbiotic relationship, we chose on the basis of intelligence. In the case of the cat, the

87

Siamese. With the dog, the Poodle and Vizsla. Boy is a Vizsla."

"I've never heard of the breed," Ronny said unhappily. "But even if I had, I doubt if they talk on Earth. You must be one hell of a trainer."

The other smiled, as though Ronny was making a joke. He said, "The Vizsla is one of the oldest breeds. They came with the Magyars from the steppes of Siberia to Europe. They were originally war dogs, then hunting hounds, and are the most versatile of all. They were pointers as well as retrievers and would hunt any game from birds to wild boar, to elk, or bear, for that matter."

"That was a long time ago," Boy said. "There's nothing to hunt on Einstein."

Dorn Horsten said, "But... but, this talking."

The other shrugged. "Man has had the dog for as long as we can trace him back. The relationship has become almost a necessity. However, we found it inconvenient for our pets to be so very less intelligent than we. So we performed genetic surgery and altered their DNA to produce a voice box, and upgraded their intelligence considerably through selective breeding and other devices."

He seemed to think that was sufficient explanation.

Ronny stared at Boy, who was lying there on the floor, his tongue dangling out the side of his mouth.

Ronny said, "I've always liked dogs. I'd give my right arm for..."

"The animal is yours," Fredric said.

Ronny boggled at him. He said, "Oh, really, now. That's very kind of you, but..."

"What's the matter?" Boy said. "Don't you want

88

me?" Aside from a guttural quality, his voice tone was quite good and very understandable.

Fredric said, "Think nothing of it. Dogs are a hobby of mine but I have quite a few and was planning to dispense with some of them. Boy is one of the few I've ever taught Amer-English. The others speak our version of Esperanto. He even reads Amer-English quite well, though his taste in novels is atrocious."

"But, well in my whole life I never expected a dog like Boy to belong to me."

"We'll soon find out who belongs to whom," the dog muttered.

"Good. It's done," Fredric said. "None of the others of the committee have shown up as yet, eh?"

The dog had got up, walked over to Ronny, gave his leg a good smell, seemed to approve, and stretched out at his feet.

Dorn Horsten said, "Rosemary has been kind enough to inform us of some of your usages. She mentioned that you have no officials on Einstein. But this committee of yours? Aren't you officials?"

"Oh, no. Not in the ordinary sense of the word. We're a temporary committee elected to meet this particular situation. That is, to answer any questions you might wish to ask about Einstein, or to show you anything you might wish to see."

"Who elected you?" Ronny said.

The other scowled slightly at him, as though the question didn't make much sense. "Why, the people."

"All of the people?"

"All who bothered to vote."

Dorn Horsten pushed his glasses further back on

the bridge of his nose. He said, "Well, who nominated you, Citizen Fredric?"

"Just Fredric," the other said. "Anyone who wished to."

Ronny had reached down to give the dog's back a scratch and was rewarded with a double wag of the tail. He said, "That's not very clear. Would you elucidate?"

"Certainly. When the news was released that you were on your way, it became obvious that there would have to be a committee. The computers were consulted as to what citizens would be best suited to act. Then our people nominated whomever they wished. The twelve who received the most nominations were put up for the vote. Those of us who were interested voted and the six who received the largest number of votes became the committee."

"How did Rosemary get into the act?" Ronny said.

Fredric looked at him, and said, "We of the committee selected her."

"Let's go back for a moment," Dorn Horsten said. "You said all of the people, and Rosemary have already mentioned that you have complete sexual equality. But what is the minimum age of the electorate?"

"There is none."

Ronny frowned. "You mean a ten year old child can vote in your elections?"

"If he or she so wishes. Usually a child of that age has little interest in elections, or has insufficient knowledge of whatever subject is being considered. But if the vote is being taken on some subject in which he is interested and has an opinion, why yes, he can and does vote."

Ronny shook his head. This was a new one. He said, "To return to this no-officials thing. You've got to have at least some officials to run your government."

The other shook his head. "Didn't Rosemary tell you? We have no government."

While the two Section G agents were gawking at him, Rosemary walked in. She was attired in practically identical clothing to that she had worn the day before and she made a little yawn before smiling her bright smile. "Good morning, Dorn and Ronny. Good morning, Fredric. Did everyone sleep well?" Without waiting for an answer, she departed into the dining room, obviously in search of coffee herself.

Ronny said, "No government! Do you mean that yours is an anarchist socio-economic system? It's one thing for a backward agricultural society such as Kropotkin to have no government. But Einstein would seem to be one of the most advanced worlds, economically, scientifically, technologically and so forth. You can't run a society like this without a government."

Fredric sipped at his coffee. "Yes, you can," he said mildly.

Dorn Horsten shook his head in amazement. He said, "And you have no president, no premier, no king or other head of state?"

"We don't have a state, let alone a head of state."

The dog looked up from where he'd had his head resting on his paws, cocked his ears forward a little, and said in a half growl, "Somebody is coming."

10

The newcomers were two women. Fredric and the Section G operatives came to their feet.

To Ronny's surprise, both of them were as attractive as Rosemary, though ten or fifteen years her senior. They wore their hair in much the same manner she did, obviously more interested in comfort than anything else. One was a redhead, the other a jet-black brunette, who looked as though she was at least half Negro. If Rosemary had reminded Ronny of that motion picture beauty of yesteryear, Jean Simmons, this one reminded him of Lena Horne of the same period. She was a knockout. They both wore approximately the same outfit that Rosemary did, blouse and kilt, though they differed in color.

They had entered from the patio and now advanced, smiling. These people did one hell of a lot of smiling, Ronny decided, even as he shook hands with them.

The redhead said, "My name's Barbara," and the brunette flashed perfect teeth and said, "And mine's Mattie."

Fredric said, "And, of course, these are our visitors, Doctor Dorn Horsten and Ronald Bronston. Dorn and Ronny, by our custom."

Rosemary came back in bearing a tray with sugar, milk, cups, spoons, and a vacuum pot of coffee.

She said, "Hello, Mattie, Barbara. Won't everybody sit down? And who would like coffee? Or anything else for that matter."

Even before they had settled, the three remaining members of the committee arrived, two men and a woman.

They were introduced, Darlene, Max and Marvin, and were soon organized.

They were all extremely handsome, Ronny decided. Rosemary had been correct when she said that on Einstein they bred for physical as well as mental attributes. Marvin seemed to be the youngest, at possibly forty. The six of the committee seemed to run from forty to fifty-five. On the youngish side, as government officials went, but, then, they had pointed out that they weren't government officials.

Settled again, spaced out very informally, Fredric said, "I suggest that we elect a chairman."

Darlene, who was an older edition of Rosemary, and just as attractive, in a more mature way, said, "You asked for it. I nominate Fredric."

"Second," Mattie said.

"Any more nominations?" Barbara said.

Evidently there were none. On the face of it, nobody gave a damn who the chairman was. The vote was unanimous.

All sipped their coffee for a moment.

Dorn Horsten politely said to Marvin, "That's a beautiful ring you have. Looks something like an Earth-side opal. One of the Australian black opals. I've always admired them."

Marvin took it off and handed it over to the doctor. He said, "Yes, our Einstein opals are

93

basically quite similar of those of Earth. They aren't a crystalline body, of course, but an amorphous mass of hydrous silica, which, in solidifying from a jelly-like state, is penetrated by cracks, these later becoming filled with material differing in water content from the original material and hence of different density. It becomes a beautiful gem. We don't have the fire opal here, such as I know is a product of Mother Earth, but our black opals are, in all modesty, superior to those of Australia and what was once called Czechoslovakia."

He had lost Ronny way back.

Dorn examined the ring appreciatively and said, "It is certainly one of the most beautiful gems I have ever seen." He handed it back towards its owner.

"It is yours," Marvin said.

Dorn Horsten ogled him. "Don't be ridiculous."

"But it is."

Dorn said, "See here. On Earth, or a dozen other worlds that I can think of, I could sell this jewel and retire for the rest of my life. It's priceless."

"Yes, of course."

Dorn shook his head. "We seem to be talking about two different things. I meant that this opal is extremely valuable and that..."

"It has no value whatsoever, on Einstein. It's priceless."

Ronny joined with Dorn in gaping at him. Ronny Bronston knew precious little about precious stones but this one was obviously a gem that a Byzantine emperor would have been proud of.

Marvin said, a bit uncomfortably, "I suppose that this is the purpose of our getting together. You wish to learn something of the workings of Einstein before our admission into United Planets. What I meant was that in our society nothing has exchange value since we produce for use rather than for sale with a view to profit. So far as exchange value is concerned, the stone is worth neither more nor less than this shirt I wear, or this house which we are in."

The two Section G agents tried to assimilate that. In their time they had been on worlds with some truly off-beat socio-economic systems.

Dorn and Ronny looked at each other.

Dorn said, "Can you think of anything else to ask, immediately?"

Ronny thought about it for a moment before looking at Rosemary and saying, "Yes. When we first met, you called me the *notorious* Ronny Bronston. Ronny *is* my nickname, but how could you have known that?" He turned his eyes to Fredric and said, "You called me the *famed* Ronald Bronston. Famed for what?"

Darlene chirped a charming laugh. "We're not as uniformed as all that. Of all humanity, you and one other Bureau of Investigation agent, Phil Birdman, are the only ones ever to have landed on a Dawnworld Planet . . . and survived."

Dorn Horsten and Ronny Bronston suddenly went cold and hard.

"Not exactly," Ronny said finally. "The others were brainwashed. Where and what did you hear about the Dawnworld Planets?"

Dorn added flatly, "Their very existence is top secret."

11

It all came back to Ronny Bronston.

He had been a First Grade Agent at the time when a small exploratory task force came upon the planets where the monkey-sized intelligent life forms originated. They had inhabited twelve planets in three star system. It had been determined that theirs was a life form which breathed an oxygen-nitrogen combination, as did man, but when found their worlds all had a methane-hydrogen-ammonia atmosphere. In short, poison gas. It would seem that some other advanced race had completely destroyed them.

It was obvious, too, that the race beyond the small intelligent life form was far from benevolent. Ross Metaxa had taken a chance and summoned the heads of state of the most advanced worlds belonging to the United Planets and revealed to them the true nature of Section G and how it had been subverting Articles One and Two of the United Planets Charter in order to prod mankind into all-out progress.

It had been a mistake. It was found that man will not necessarily unite in the face of a common danger if his political, socioeconomic or religious institutions are threatened. *Better dead than red*, had been the American slogan back in the 20th Century when the whole world had been faced with nuclear holocaust; and the Russians had similar slogans about capitalism.

Some of the member planets had immediately dropped out of the confederation, and Ross Metaxa was afraid that if the story spread, and the more backward worlds found that their institutions had been tampered with by Section G, that they would desert *en masse*.

Indeed, the ambitious Supreme Commandant of the militaristically inclined planet Phrygia, Baron Maximilian Wyler, had taken off almost immediately in his space yacht and headed home. And it was soon found that he dominated Interplanetary Press, the news service.

Metaxa had dispatched Ronny Bronston under vague orders to do whatever could be done to shut up the Baron.

On the way, Ronny had become acquainted with Rita Daniels, niece of the dictator of Phrygia, who had dropped information indicating just how ambitious Wyler was.

On Phrygia he had found that there was only one other Section G agent there, Phil Birdman, of Indian descent and originally from the planet Piegan. Birdman had accumulated information that indicated that Baron Wyler was eager to attack his neighboring worlds and to form an empire.

Ronny had gotten in touch with Metaxa and Jakes and made arrangements for him to be named a plenipotentiary extraordinary from United Planets to the Supreme Commandant of Phrygia. The Baron evidently had some of his heavies out looking for Ronny Bronston, and Ronny wanted to throw around some weight.

Metaxa saw it through. The president had declared Ronny a special mission to Baroy Wyler and Sid Jakes had notified the Supreme Commandant that Ronald Bronston was on his way.

The reception had been more than impressive. Above ground, the Baron's palace was a replica of that of King Minos' Knossos, complete with guards in Cretan armor, even to chariots. Below ground, it was the height of modernity.

Ronny had been whisked to the Supreme Commandant's personal quarters in the bowels of the building. When the elevator door had opened, he was confronted by a tall, heavy-set man, his face beaming and his hand extended for a hearty shake. Baron Wyler carried his weight well; gracefully might be the better word. He moved as a trained pugilist moves, or perhaps one of the larger cats. His charm reached out and embraced you, all but suffocating you. His face was open; his eyes, blue and wide-set; his arched Hapsburg nose giving an aristocratic quality that only his overwhelming friendliness could dissipate.

Ronny had been taken to as comfortable a room as the Section G agent could ever remember having been in and there had been surprised to find that Wyler had a complete dossier on him down to the most intimate facts.

He also had some startling information. His space fleet had landed on the worlds of the small life forms and, wearing gas masks, had gathered up what information they could. This included a star chart of the some hundred of what the Baron called the Dawnman Worlds and of various films and tapes which had obviously been taken on these worlds.

He showed one of these films to Ronny, in particular a close-up of one of the Dawnmen. "But that's a human being!" Ronny had blurted.

The Dawnman was incredibly handsome. He was dressed in nothing more than brief shorts and sandals. He had a golden-brown coloration, was of bodily perfection seldom seen and then only among physical culture perfectionists who spend a lifetime achieving it. He could have stepped off a pedestal in a Greek temple devoted to the god Apollo. He seemed to be about six and a half feet tall and to weigh about one hundred and ninety. His hair was dark cream, his eyes were blue and very clear and there was the slightest of smiles on his lips. There was no indication that he was aware of being photographed.

Baron Wyler had told Ronny that evidently the technology of the Dawnworlds was incredibly advanced. They had such things as nuclear fusion, and, hence, unlimited power, and matter conversion units that could make anything out of anything. But, said the Baron, there was just one thing in which the Dawnmen differed from man. These aliens didn't seem to be intelligent.

Ronny had bugeyed him and Baron Wyler had summoned one of his top scientists, the elderly Academecian Count Felix Fitzjames to help explain. He had dubbed this alien culture the Dawnmen because there was a hypothesis that man had originated there and that Earth had been seeded from one of their planets, that Cro-Magnon man was of the same stock.

The academician explained why it was possible that the Dawnmen were not intelligent. Given a

99

creature with a voicebox and a hand suitable for using tools and, even though his intelligence was low, in a few megayears, bit by bit, he would accumulate knowledge and know-how until in time even matter converters would be his to utilize.

Count Fitzjames had gone on to compare the Dawnworlds with the caste system of India. The Aryan invaders of the sub-continent had been afraid that unless they took stringent measures, they would soon interbreed with the more numerous indigenous people to the point of merging with them. So they divided society into four orders: the Brahmins, who kept up religious and scholarly pursuits; the Kshatriyas, who were the ruling class and warriors; and the Vaishyas, traders and businessmen. All these were composed of the conquering Aryans. Intermarriage between castes was forbidden—a deep religious matter. Below these three castes were the Sudras, which were composed of the original peoples and took over the laboring jobs. Beneath these were the outcastes, the untouchables, who were consigned to the most menial tasks. According to the academician, under the caste system the Indians had made many of the important breakthroughs of the human race, such as discovering the zero in mathematics, at a time when most Europeans were running about in animal skins.

He pointed out that under such a system a man who belonged to, say, the cobbler caste, would pass on his trade to his descendents. It would never occur to them to do anything but make shoes, any more than it would occur to a Brahmin *not* to get the best education available. After a few thousand years, the cobbler caste would be turning out some superlative shoes, and after a few megayears at it they would instinctively make shoes. It would become a matter of genetics. Over the megayears, the inadequate shoemakers, the throwbacks, would have been weeded out. It would be similar to the bees who need no training to collect honey, or the soldier ant to guard the ant community. In short, a ritual-taboo society.

After the Count had left, Baron Wyler had explained to Ronny why he had revealed all this information. He was ambitious to achieve in actuality what Section G had been working on for a century or more, that is a *real* United Planets, a strong progressive United Planets—under his banner, of course. To achieve this, he needed good men, such as Ronny, on his team.

Ronny pointed out that it would seem unlikely that even such a militarily inclined a world as Phrygia could take on all 2435 other worlds of United Planets. But the Baron had merely smiled and told him they had the star chart that revealed the location of the Dawnman worlds. Given one of those matter converters, nothing could stand in his way. His scientists could duplicate it in any size, and overnight he would have at his command a fleet of space cruisers that would dwarf the combined might of the whole confederation.

Taken aback, Ronny had said he'd think it over and returned to the quarters of Phil Birdman where he immediately got in touch with Metaxa and Sid Jakes. Metaxa, obviously hating to say it, told Ronny he must get hold of that star chart. They had to know the location of the Dawnworlds.

There was only one thing to do. Either he or

Birdman had to go into pseudo-time and enter the palace. Undoubtedly, the chart would be near the Baron since he was obviously working night and day on his project. Birdman protested that he was already forty-five years of age and going into pseudo-time for any protracted period took at least fifteen years off your life. Ronny was only thirty-two so he took on the job.

They drove to the palace and parked before the main entry and Ronny slipped a syrette into his arm. Within moments, the world seemingly stopped. All movement stopped. Munching energy pills as fast as he could, he dashed for the underground living quarters of the Baron. He found the Baron, stock-still as was everybody else, in conference with some of his military leaders, and, after difficulties, found the chart and dashed back with it, still desperately bolting energy pills which were having less and less effect on him.

They started back for town, the Baron's security guards close behind, and knew that they wouldn't make it. Luck intervened and on the way they met Rita Daniels and abducted her as a hostage, since she was the Baron's favorite relative.

Knowing that the Baron would undoubtedly immediately head for the Dawnworlds, before the United Planets Space Fleet could intervene, Ronny and Birdman, under Metaxa's orders, summoned a space cruiser and, still holding Rita Daniels as a hostage, set off for the nearest Dawnworld themselves.

Captain Gary Volos and his three officers of the Space Cruiser *Pisa* had at first given them trouble, thinking they were challenging Articles One and

Two of the Charter, in abducting the niece of a head of state, but when the Dawnman planet was reached they had come around. They had soon detected Baron Wyler's space yacht and Ronny landed to reconnoiter.

The planet was one large garden with nothing resembling a city to be seen. However, Ronny had soon stumbled upon a group of the Dawnmen, obviously having a picnic. They completely ignored him, as though he simply wasn't there. With them, they had several coffee-grinder-looking devices which were, on the face of it, matter converters. They could pour even sand in the top and come up with fruit, wine, or whatever else they wanted.

Ronny had been tempted to steal one of them but some instinct prevented him and he refrained. He received a call from the *Pisa* and found that the Baron had got in touch with them and was requesting help.

He returned to the space cruiser and they landed next to the Baron's yacht. Ronny went over and found that only Baron Wyler and Count Fitzjames occupied the spaceship.

The Baron, a broken man, revealed that all of his crew had been sent out with orders to obtain a matter converter, and anything else that seemed desirable. They had been captured and taken to the top of a pyramid-like ancient building, placed on an altar and one by one had their hearts cut from their chests in a religious ceremony similar to that of the Aztecs.

Count Fitzjames thought he had figured it out. Using the Indian caste system again, as an example, he contended that the Dawnmen had evolved a very high industrial level, bee-hive type culture. They're a happy people, he said. Everybody is happy—or he's a genetic defective and disposed of, because he *is* a genetic defective, or he'd be happy.

They were evidently not aggressive, but were insect-like in their manner of defense of their territories and their way of doing things. They weren't aggressive since they were one hundred percent ritualistic and had no ritual for aggression. At first, he and the Baron had been amazed when they landed that the Dawnmen ignored them. But they couldn't have done anything else since they had no rituals that applied to strangers. But they did have rituals that applied to stealing, and the Baron's men had fallen victim to them. Undoubtedly the same thing had happened to the monkey-like aliens. The Dawnmen had ruthlessly destroyed their whole three star systems as a result.

A telepathic message had at that point entered the minds of the three of them. The Baron was informed that Phrygia had been destroyed. But Ronny was informed that he committed no wrong and was instructed to return to Earth and warn others away. They had scanned his body and found the result of his having gone into pseudo-time and thus shortened his life. However, so that he could spread the warning they had made rectifications on him so that he will live some two and a half centuries.

The voice-in-their-brains went on to explain that it represents the equivalent of the Brahmins on the Dawnworlds. It wound up saying, "We have no designs against you. So long as you have none against us, our cultures need never conflict. Farewell..."

Upon return to Earth, Metaxa rejected the idea of warning all human planets to stay away. He pointed out that more than one of the United Planets might react hysterically and want to go to war. Others would have elements among them that would want to steal, as the Baron had, the advanced technology. There would possibly even be religious cranks who'd want to send missionaries.

Instead, the Baron, Rita Daniels, and both crews of the space cruisers were brainwashed, so that they'd forget all they knew about the Dawnworlds. Ronny and Birdman alone were deemed safe to have the information. And Ronny, in reward for his services, was raised to supervisor rank.

12

Now Ronny was saying, "Where and what did you hear about the Dawnman Worlds?"

Fredric said, "You mentioned that the others who landed with you had been brainwashed. I don't believe I know that term. What do you mean?"

"Memory wiped," Ronny told him flatly. "All their memories about the Dawnworlds were erased."

"What an intrusion!" Mattie protested.

Ronny looked over at her. "Yes," he said. "But a necessary one. The human race is at stake."

Fredric said, "But you are trusted with the secret of the existence of the Dawnworlds, and with their location?"

"Yes. The Commissioner of Section G decided that we should have *someone* knowledgeable about them."

"And Phil Birdman?"

"Phil Birdman was killed not long ago on an assignment."

"And the Supreme Commandant of Phrygia?"

"Suicided shortly after our return from the Dawnworlds. I am the only person alive who knows their location. I burned the star chart showing it. The galaxy being as large as it is, it could take a millenium to locate them without my assistance."

His eyes narrowed. "But, once again, how do you

know about these things, the names of Birdman and the Supreme Commandant?"

Max said softly, "You left out one survivor of your adventure, Ronny Bronston. Academician Count Felix Fitzjames. After the destruction of Phrygia he did not commit suicide, as did his late commandant. He eluded your agents and came here to Einstein and requested asylum. It was granted him, in view of the fact that he was an outstanding authority in the field of anthropology."

Dorn Horsten said coldly, "Where is he now?"

Fredric took over again. "The Academician was an aged man. He is dead."

Ronny said, "And he revealed to you the location of the Dawnworlds?"

"He couldn't. He didn't know. He was an academician, not a navigator. But he told us the story of them and your activities there. We would like to know more. The story is fascinating."

"That, it is," Ronny said flatly. "It is also the most restricted story in United Planets. Not even my superiors know the location of those worlds. They don't want to. It must never get out and each additional person who knows a secret makes it that much more difficult to keep it."

Barbara, frowning slightly, said, "You of Section G seem to make an awfully big issue of this. Why?"

"Because we're afraid to death that some crackpot element will find out where they're located and go there and, as a result, doom the whole human race." He looked from one of them to the other, slowly, deliberately. "So I am not about to reveal the location of the Dawnworlds, even to citizens of the planet Einstein, no matter what their Intelligence

107

Quotient. Someone, a long time ago, pointed out that high intelligence is no guarantee of high integrity. Some of the most intelligent people who ever lived were also ambitious. The Medicis and Borgias of the Renaissance were admittedly brilliant. So was Napoleon, or he wouldn't have been the military genius he proved himself to be. No, intelligence is no guarantee of integrity, nor even a guarantee of correct decision. According to our racial legends, an omniscient God created man. A mistake if I ever heard of one."

They laughed dutifully.

Marvin said, "Academician Fitzjames informed us that the, ah, Brahmins of the Dawnworld you landed upon had, evidently telepathically, determined that your life had been shortened and, wishing to keep you alive so that you could warn others off, still, evidently, through nothing more than a telepathic contact, then extended your life for over two hundred years. In short, they have the elixir of life, as the old alchemists used to call it."

Ronny said, "Whether or not my life has been extended for over two hundred years, I don't know. I'll have to wait it out. However, it is true that my aging fifteen or twenty years overnight did not happen, though, as a result of a drug I took, it should have. But now, I'll answer no more questions about the Dawnworlds. The information is taboo. Far from warning others off, as the Brahmins wished, it was decided by Ross Metaxa not even to let others know they exist, let alone their location."

Boy got up from the floor and stretched and said, "You humans sure do a lot of yakking. I think I'll go get something to eat." He headed for the dining room and Ronny and Dorn looked after him for a moment, blankly.

Two or three of the others laughed, especially when the dog's voice came back, ordering a steak for himself at the automated table.

Ronny muttered, "I don't think I'll ever get used to that."

Dorn Horsten pushed his pince nez glasses back on the bridge of his nose and said, "To get back to the workings of the planet Einstein."

"Yes, of course," Fredric said.

"We were informed at the Octagon that, when you colonized, the basic requirement was an I.Q. of at least 130. After all these years, what is the average today?"

Fredric frowned before saying slowly, "We no longer use the I.Q. system for measuring intelligence. We couldn't, even if we wished. In the I.Q. system, what would have happened if a child answered correctly all 100 of the questions in the required time?"

Ronny said, "What methods did you utilize to upgrade your mental and physical attributes?"

Fredric said, "I am not a geneticist. However, briefly, from earliest youth a child is checked out not only for its physical attributes but its—I.Q. you would call it—and its ability quotient."

"Ability quotient?" Dorn said.

"Ability quotient is the child's performance in verbal ability, verbal fluency, numerical ability, spatial ability, perceptual ability, memory, accident proneness, digital dexterity, analogizing power, mechanical aptitude, clerical aptitude, emotional maturity, tone discrimination, taste sensitivity, sexual attraction, color blindness, accuracy, persistence, freedom from neurosis, and powers of observation."

Ronny whistled softly between his teeth.

Fredric went on. "At the age of fifteen if the child does not check out at least five percent higher than its parents in intelligence and ability quotient, it is sterilized by the Medical Department of Genetics. We wish to take no chances of the child's genes continuing."

Both Dorn and Ronny blinked a bit at that one, but Dorn said, "You utilize other methods?"

"Yes, truly outstanding examples of our males have their sperm frozen and it is used over a period of time to artificially inseminate outstanding females."

"Your methods seem somewhat drastic," Dorn said thoughtfully. "However, it is an internal matter and I rather doubt that it would be grounds to prevent you from becoming a member of United Planets."

Max said, "I think that something should be pointed out to our visitors. Our, mmm, I.Q.'s aren't as high as all that. You see, we started with a minimum of 130 and a median of, perhaps, 140 and by carefully breeding up the average five percent each generation, eliminating those who didn't upgrade, and utilizing artificial insemination from the ultra-high, each generation would develop. However, it takes little mathematics to show that in four generations, a century roughly, the median of 140 would only have increased to about 170 which is not unknown on other worlds of United Planets."

Ronny said dryly, "But it's not exactly widespread."

Barbara said, very earnestly, "You must understand that by utilizing genetic surgery to alter the DNA, as we have done on animals, we could speed up this acceleration. However, we wish to avoid generation gaps. It might be possible, overnight, to up our, uh, I.Q. to a thousand average, compared to the one hundred of Earth. But then, the older generations would not be able to associate with the new. It is one thing communicating with someone who has an I.Q. ten to twenty points higher than yours, but it is another if it is ten times as high."

Fredric had been looking at the two Section G men unhappily. He said now, "I see that you don't approve of our methods. I might point out that the need has long been expressed. Plato proposed an eugenic program, saying, 'In the same way, if we want to prevent the human race from degeneration, we shall take care to encourage union between the better elements of both sexes, and to eliminate that of the worst.'"

Darlene put in, "We minimize gene surgery, gene copying, gene insertion and gene deletion. Algeny and genetic engineering we handle with kid gloves. We utilize nature, largely, rather than science and technology to upgrade our people."

Dorn said, "What surprises me is that we have so little trouble communicating with you. I would never know that we weren't on Earth or Archimedes or one of the other advanced planets. But surely there is a great intellectual gap between us."

Marvin said, "We selected not only citizens who

111

spoke Basic and Amer-English but also those who had the widest experience with people from over-space. We six have already had considerable contact, through attending scientific conventions and through the small amount of trade we conduct with other worlds."

"I see," Ronny said, self-deprecation in his voice. "You're especially selected to meet us. Rosemary is stupid, as she put it, and hence better able to communicate with us. You've been through the ordeal before, and so are able."

Fredric was distressed. "You must not think in that manner. See here, Ronny, how would you like to submit to one of our present-day equivalents of an I.Q. test, just to see where you stand as compared to the average Einstein citizen?"

"Hell no," Ronny said. "It'd probably give me an inferiority complex that'd last the rest of my life."

"But surely such an organization as your own required a high I.Q. before you were admitted."

"Possibly, but I still don't want to compare mine with yours, any more than I'd want to compare my last dog with Boy. It would have given Gimmick the willies even to come in contact with Boy."

And so it went. Ronny Bronston and Dorn Horsten fired every question they could think of at the six-member committee, pertaining to the workings of Einstein. They pried further into the socioeconomic system. They delved into its govern-mental system, or its lack of it. They asked about religion and found that there was none. They had gotten into quite a discussion on the difference between accumulated knowledge and intelligence.

It was pointed out by Max that Einstein was as

desperately at work accumulating knowledge as it was increasing intelligence. One was meaningless without the other.

They took out time for lunch and Rosemary suggested that the guests from over-space might like to sample dishes which had originated on Einstein and wines that had been developed on this world.

It was delicious beyond belief.

After lunch, they returned to the living room with coffee and a local dessert wine and had at it again. It wasn't necessary for Ronny and Dorn to consult with each other to realize that both were coming to the same conclusion. Ross Metaxa's fears were meaningless. There was no reason at all why Einstein should not be admitted into United Planets. Indeed, it was fast becoming increasingly obvious that she was the most advanced world ever settled by humanity. Einstein was exactly the kind of member planet that they needed most. Undoubtedly, she had made thousands of scientific and technological discoveries that could be assimilated by other worlds.

Arrangements were made for Dorn Horsten to meet some of the scientists in his particular field the following day, and arrangements for Ronny to visit the Einstein version of a university. It would seem schools on this world were unlike any elsewhere. They had revolutionized education as much as they had any other field.

During one break, Dorn had drifted over to Rosemary's bar to refresh his glass.

Barbara, the gorgeous redhead, came over, her own glass in hand and smiled into his eyes. She said, "I was wondering if you would like a bed companion tonight. I don't believe I've ever seen a man as large as you before. It rather excites me."

Dorn Horsten kept himself from gaping at her, and then swallowed. He adjusted his pince-nez glasses on his nose. It was one of the reasons he wore the antiquated things. It gave you a chance to do something for a moment, while your mind raced to accommodate the unexpected.

He said gallantly, "I was just in the process of screwing up my courage to the point of asking you." He made a slight bow.

"Good," she smiled. "I'll spend the night here with you, then. The others have been invited to stay at Fredric's place. He lives quite near."

The day sped by under the impetus of fascinating discoveries and, before they knew it, they were at table again.

It was a yawning Ronny Bronston by the time they split up, and all of the committee save Barbara took off for Fredric's home. Nobody seemed to think twice about Barbara remaining. As Dorn had thought the night before, they had no sexual taboos whatsoever. He suspected that had he asked one or more of the other women to stay as well, they most likely would have taken him up.

Boy followed Ronny to his suite and looked about it while his new master began wearily shedding his clothes.

The dog said, "Not bad, as human tastes go. What bed do you sleep in?"

"This one," Ronny said, sitting down on it to remove his shoes.

"Then I'll take this one," Boy told him and jumped up on it and stretched out.

114

Ronny looked over at the dog and shook his head in continued amazement. He said, "Boy, how old are you?"

"I'll be five in a few weeks. That's Einstein calendar, of course. I don't know what it'd be Earth-calendar."

"A human child of five wouldn't have your vocabulary. Not on Earth, at least."

"Not on Einstein, either," Boy said, then let his tongue hang out long enough for three quick pants. "We mature more quickly. A human isn't even sexually mature until he reaches up to fifteen. Hell, I had my first bitch when I was only one. A cute poodle."

Ronny shook his head again and returned to his shoes.

There came a knock at the door and, without waiting for his response, Rosemary entered, her smile bright as always. She carried a bottle and two champagne glasses.

"Nightcap," she announced.

"Wizard," Ronny said. Inwardly, he was hoping that she wouldn't be quite so much of a barracuda tonight. He had done nothing but talk all day, but he was tired. Come to think of it, he was still sexually tired from the night before.

She put the two glasses down on the room's center table and began expertly to draw the cork. She popped it and, just as expertly, poured before the effervescent wine could overflow the bottle.

Boy said, accusingly, "You didn't bring a bowl for me. I've got a taste for bubbly wine."

She looked over at him, as though seeing him for the first time. She said, apologetically, "Oh, Ronny,

I couldn't possibly... well, I couldn't do anything with a dog watching us."

"Who wants to watch?" Boy growled. "What do you think I am, some sort of voyeur?"

She said, "I'm sorry, Boy."

"All right, all right," he said, getting up and jumping off the bed. "I'll go sleep in the living room." He looked at Ronny and it was absolutely possible to see disgust in his expression. "This is a hell of a way to start our relationship, Boss." And with that, he trotted out.

"Sorry, Boy," Ronny said apologetically after him.

After the dog was gone, Rosemary said, "It's just a thing I have. I can't bear to have intelligent animals watching me when I make love." She handed Ronny one of the two glasses and began to undress.

He sipped appreciatively, then finished the sparkling wine in two gulps and rolled over into the bed. The whole group of them had been drinking, off and on, since lunch and he didn't need any more—especially if he was going to perform with the beauteous Rosemary. Alcohol had a tendency to slow him down in bed.

She said, "I was fascinated by what you said about those Dawnman planets. Are they very far away?"

He said, his mind as weary as his body, "Yes. And in a direction that's such that I doubt if man, at his current rate of expansion, would ordinarily touch into the area for another millenium."

"Why would that be?" she said, slipping out of her kilt.

"Different spiral," he yawned. "You know, Earth is rather far out, you might say on the outskirts of the galaxy, in an area rather sparsely occupied by sun

116

systems, compared to closer in to the center. With billions of sun systems involved, even with the under-space drive, our race could take an almost unbelievable time to expand to the point where we ran into the Dawnworld culture, or other intelligent life, for that matter." He thought about it. "But it's only a matter of time, of course. Sooner or later we will—unless we lose our drive to expand."

She kicked off her Etruscan revival slippers. "So the Dawnworlds are closer in toward the center?"

"That's right," he told her, "but I shouldn't even be talking about it."

She said, "What's all this about their being so advanced but that they're not really intelligent? That doesn't sound very reasonable."

"It's that same discussion we had earlier. About intelligence and accumulated knowledge. If you had an intelligence half, or even a quarter, of the average on Earth, not to speak of Einstein, in a few megayears you'd have one hell of a lot of accumulated knowledge. You wouldn't have to be smart. In a few million years you would have figured out one hell of a lot of things, assuming, obviously, that you had enough wit to develop a written language as well as a spoken one, so you could pass your accumulated material on to the next generation."

She climbed into bed next to him but didn't immediately act as frankly as she had the night before. She simply stretched out, there, and put her hands behind her head. "In what direction, toward the center of the galaxy, are they?" she said idly.

And alarm bells rang in his head.

But it was then that the knockout drops hit Ronny Bronston.

13

Dorn Horsten was awakened in the morning by Boy licking his face.

He sat up abruptly, sputtering.

"What...what..."

Boy said, "The Boss is gone."

"What do you mean, gone?" Dorn blurted, still half asleep.

"He's not in his suite."

Dorn Horsten reached over to the night table and got his glasses and put them on and then stared at the dog. "Well, where did he go?"

"I don't know. I wasn't there. Rosemary doesn't like dogs watching when she's making love. I slept in the living room on the couch."

Dorn shook his head in an effort to drive the remains of sleep away. "Is she gone, too? Maybe they took a walk, or something." He was speaking in whispers, so as not to awaken the redhead on the pillow beside him.

"She's still there, sleeping like a log. She didn't even wake up when I licked her."

The Section G agent swung his feet over the side of the bed. Barbara, his bedmate, continued to sleep on, in spite of the talk. No wonder. They'd had quite a siege of it the night before. The woman had seemed insatiable. He reached over for his trousers and struggled into them, then, without even shoes, headed for the door. "Come along," he said to the dog.

They entered Ronny's suite without knocking. Rosemary was still stretched out, nude, on the bed.

Among other degrees, Dorn Horsten held an M.D. He stared down at her for a moment, then reached out and with his fingers opened one of her eyes.

"Drugged," he muttered. He slapped her face back and forth for a moment.

Finally, she awakened, looking groggy. "Whaz amatter?"

Dorn said urgently, "Where's Ronny?"

She vaguely looked over at the pillow next to hers. It was, of course, empty.

"Why...why, I don't know."

"He's not here," Dorn said urgently, "and you've been drugged."

"Drugged!" Suddenly, she was more alert. Her eyes went about the room searchingly. "But...that's impossible."

He looked around too. "How could it have been administered? I ate everything and drank everything that you two did, and I haven't been drugged."

She shook her head. "I simply don't know."

"Did you two eat or drink anything, after you left the rest of us?"

"No. No, of course not."

The dog looked at her strangely, but didn't say anything. He also looked about the room. There was no sign of the bottle of champagne and the two glasses.

"Come on," Dorn said to him. "Let's search the rest of the house."

119

They went through every room of the underground building, finding exactly nothing and finally winding up in the patio's center.

"Maybe he went for a walk," the big man said, knowing full well that was nonsense.

"And maybe he didn't," the dog growled. "She's lying. Either that, or she's so dopey she's forgotten."

Dorn glowered at him. "What in the name of the Holy Ultimate are you talking about?"

Boy said, "Last night, she came into the room with a bottle of wine and two glasses in way of a nightcap. Then she objected to my sticking around, so I left. The bottle and the glasses aren't there now."

Dorn muttered something and returned to his own suite. Barbara was still in the bed, out like a light. He wondered if she, too, was drugged, but doubted it; her breathing sounded perfectly normal. He got into the rest of his clothes and his shoes and headed for the living room, Boy trailing after.

He sat at the center table and brought forth his communicator and propped it up before him and activated it. Irene Kasansky's face faded in, looking harassed, as usual.

Dorn said, "Is the Old Man available?"

"No. He's gone over to London for some sort of confab. What's up?"

"How about Sid Jakes?"

"He's in conference. What's wrong?"

"Get him out of conference. Ronny's been nabbed."

Her eyes widened. "What the Holy Ultimate are you talking about? The assignment you're on is a milk run. What could possibly go wrong?"

"I don't know," Dorn said emptily.

She flicked a switch, and shortly Sid Jake's face beamed out at him from the small phone screen of the communicator.

"Dorn!" he said happily. "How's it going? Having a good time? I envy you field men. I haven't had a vacation since..."

Dorn Horsten interrupted him. "Something's developed here that doesn't make sense. We've only been here two days but the night before last, I caught two men searching my luggage. They got away. Last night, Ronny disappeared. His bedmate was drugged and he's simply gone."

"Bedmate?" Sid Jakes chortled. "You've been there only two days and already he's sleeping with some mopsy? Ronny's a fast operator."

"I've got one too," Dorn growled. "But the thing is this. Remember that Count Felix Fitzjames, the top scientist from Phrygia? Well, when he disappeared before we could brainwash him, he didn't exactly disappear. He came here to Einstein and they took him in. He told them all he knew about the Dawnworlds, and he probably knew as much about them as anybody did, including Ronny. There was only one thing he couldn't tell them. Where they're located. Nobody living knows that...except Ronny."

For once, Sid Jakes' face was less than happy. He said, "Oh, wizard. I can see it coming."

"Yes. Somebody on this brainworld has got hold of Ronny and it's only a matter of time before they put him under Scop or some other truth serum, and he tells them where the Dawnmen are."

"Why should they care?"

"How would I know?"

121

Sid Jakes closed his eyes in pain. "Otherwise, how are they, there on Einstein?"

"Very advanced, very reasonable, in an off-beat sort of way. I can't see any reason for keeping them out of the United Planets, or any way of doing it when it's put to a vote among the member worlds."

Sid Jakes opened his eyes and said, "Find him. Find Ronny, Horsten. Find him before they get the secret from him."

"How?" Dorn Horsten said plaintively.

"How would I know? You're there, I'm not. But whoever has nabbed Ronny, as you put it, can't be allowed to have the information about the location of the Dawnmen. Take whatever steps necessary. You're a trouble shooter. Start shooting."

"And if I have to take rugged ones, tough steps? Section G backs me to the hilt?"

"Don't be silly," Sid Jakes snorted. "If your methods get too rugged, we won't even admit knowing you exist." His face faded, glowing a sardonic grin.

Dorn Horsten closed his own eyes in mute agony.

He opened them and looked at Boy. He said, "I haven't been out of this house since we came to Einstein. How in the name of the Holy Ultimate am I supposed to find Ronny Bronston?"

The dog hung his tongue out of his mouth and for three quick pants, wagged his bobbed tail twice and said, "What do you think I've got this nose for?"

"Nose?"

"Nose."

"How do you mean?"

The dog had been stretched out on the floor. Now he arose. "Come along," he said. "We'll trail the Boss."

Dorn Horsten hesitantly followed him. All his inclinations were to get into immediate touch with Fredric and the other members of the committee. On the face of it, they couldn't be part of the conspiracy. Had they wanted to question Ronny about the location of the Dawnworlds they wouldn't have had to abduct him. They could have taken him, there at the spaceport, and injected him with the truth serum, Scop, then and there. Besides, after the day-long conversations they'd had, he couldn't believe the six committee members could be Machiavellian. However, how had Ronny put it? High intelligence was no guarantee of integrity.

He followed the Vizsla back to the door of Ronny's suite and the dog scurried around the room sniffing. Then he hung his tongue out several inches, turned and trotted toward the patio, then the entry to the underground house, his nose near the ground.

"They went this way," he said.

"Who's they?" Dorn said, hurrying to keep up.

"Two men and the Boss. I think they're carrying him. I got the scent of all three of them at the door, but now only the two strangers. I'm trailing them."

They went through the entry and emerged into the golf course-like countryside.

Dorn said, in disgust, "By this time, they'll be miles from here."

The dog, still sniffing along, said, "No, they won't. They won't be far at all. The Boss isn't very big but he's still big enough that they won't be figuring on carrying him very far."

"Surely they've got a vehicle."

"I doubt it. On Einstein, all cars are automated. The computers know, at any given time, the location of every one on the planet. If they had a car and it picked them up at this point, then all we'd have to do is check with the computers and they'd let us know where it went. So they can't afford to use a car. Besides, I can still get their scent. They went this way."

He set off at a fairly good clip and Dorn had to trot to keep up.

The dog panted, "When we catch them, you're going to have to do the dirty work. I'm conditioned, programmed not to attack any inhabitant of Einstein."

"It'll be a pleasure," the big man said grimly. "Is there any chance they're armed? On a romp like this, they probably would be."

"No," the dog said. "There are no arms on Einstein. I've read about them, but I've never seen a gun."

Twice they passed over narrow roads of the type utilized by hover-craft and once Dorn discerned the entry to one of the underground houses.

They hadn't come more than half a kilometer before Boy said, I think this is it." He darted around a small hill, followed by the big scientist at a trot. There was an entry there.

"This is it, all right," Boy panted. "Here's where you take over, Doc."

They pounded through the entry and into a patio beyond. It was fairly similar to that of Rosemary, but there was one notable difference. The windows were decoratively covered with wrought iron bars.

A voice shouted, "Halt." Dorn spun to confront the voice. Two young men were racing toward him.

They were huskies, though not in Dorn Horsten's category. He slipped his glasses from his nose and

124

into a side pocket and reached out and grabbed just as they were about to dash into him.

With deceptive speed he banged their heads together. They both reeled for a dazed moment, then fell.

"Holy smokes," the dog said in admiration. "Some Doc you turned out to be."

They hurried over to the main door. It was locked.

"They took him through here," Boy said, his tongue hanging out again, his stubby tail wagging in appreciation of the excitement.

It was a heavy door, studded with wrought iron, in keeping with the rest of the patio's decor. Dorn hesitated not for a moment. He hit it crushingly with the butt of his right hand and it crashed inward, the hinges screeching protest as they ripped from the wall.

Dorn darted through, counting on surprise if there were any others inside. He trusted the dog, but couldn't be sure about the presence of weapons in the hands of the enemy. Even though such were not manufactured on Einstein, it was always possible to import them secretly.

The door opened up onto a large living room and there were two more men seated there. Their eyes boggled when the oversized Dorn Horsten came charging in, followed by Boy.

"These are the two that had the Boss," the dog said.

They immediately scrambled to their feet to meet the big scientist's attack. They might have saved themselves the trouble. He hit each one exactly once and though he had pulled his punches, both went down as though struck by lightning.

Boy was running around sniffing. "The boss is over this way, I think," he said excitedly, heading for a door at the far end of the room. Dorn followed.

The door wasn't locked and they went through it in orthodox fashion. It was a bedroom and Ronny was stretched out on the bed, fully clothed, including shoes.

Dorn skidded to a halt. He didn't like how his colleague looked.

"How are you?" he demanded.

Ronny said slowly, his eyes focusing poorly, "I'm... under... scop."

"Holy Ultimate," Dorn said in protest. "You shouldn't give truth serum to a drugged man. Have they questioned you yet?"

"Yes."

"Did you tell them the location of the Dawn-worlds?"

"Yes."

"Oh, wizard," the big man said, his shoulders slumping. "Now the fat's in the fire."

14

Dorn Horsten bent over Ronny. He said, "Who are they?"

"I ... don't ... know."

"We better get out of here. Maybe more of them might show up, and it's just possible some of them might be armed. Can you walk?"

"I ... think ... so."

"Then get up and let's get out of here."

Under the Scop, Ronny couldn't have disobeyed if he had wanted to. He swung his legs over the side of the bed and came erect, a bit woozily.

Dorn picked up a small packet from the side of the bed, scowled at it, then slipped it into his pocket.

Boy had been standing guard at th door. Now he looked over a shoulder and said, "Hello, Boss. You look like hell. This'll teach you to run me out of the room and leave you alone with a bitch."

Dorn scowled at the dog. "What do you mean?"

"Who else could have slipped the boss that dope?"

"She was drugged, too."

"Sure. First she gave it to the Boss. Then she got rid of the bottle and glasses after taking a slug of the stuff herself, and climbed back into bed. She figured that'd make her free from suspicion. She was too high and mightily superior to think of me being able to point the paw of suspicion at her."

"Hmmm," Dorn said, taking Ronny by the arm to steady him. "We'll see about it."

They cautiously left the room, noted that the two kidnappers Dorn had slugged were still out cold, and crossed to the broken door of the patio, the big man still supporting the wobbly Ronny Bronston. The two men whose heads he had cracked together were also still not of this world.

They got down the entry way and outside and started back toward Rosemary's house. There was simply no other place to go.

Dorn said, "We'll make better time this way," and took up the smaller agent and slung him over his shoulder and broke into a longer stride.

Boy began ranging, checking on possible pursuit, or possible ambush ahead or to the side. For a large dog, he was fast.

The effects of Scop don't last very long," Dorn said. "How long have you had it in you?"

"About...an...hour..."

"It'll be wearing off by the time we get back to the house. Did they ask you any other questions?"

"No."

"That's what they were after, all right," Dorn said grimly. "And they got it. The location of the Dawnworlds. Why do they want it?"

"I...don't...know."

They arrived back at Rosemary's house without pursuit or further incident. In the patio, Dorn Horsten put his fellow-agent back onto his feet. Ronny wasn't nearly as groggy now, and his speech came more clearly.

"Let's go see Rosemary," he said. "I got those knockout drops in some wine she gave me."

They headed for his suite, initially.

Dorn said, "She was drugged too. Possibly someone else got to that wine."

"Ha," Boy said and was even able to get a tone of sarcasm into his voice."

Ronny said grimly, "I saw her pop the cork. And she turned her back to me while she was pouring it."

Somewhat to Dorn's surprise, they found Rosemary still in bed. He had expected her to be up and around by now, and in some other part of the house.

Dorn entered the room first and blocked her seeing Ronny with his huge build.

She saw the look on his face and said, "I have a raging headache, evidently from that drug. I thought I'd stay..." Then she saw Ronny Bronston and her eyes widened. "Ronny!" she said. "What happened?"

He looked at her thoughtfully.

Dorn Horsten brought the small packet from his side pocket and opened it. He brought something from it and then quickly bent over her, grabbed a resisting arm and slipped a syrette into it.

She tried to pull away. "What's that!" she demanded, her eyes fearful.

"Scop," Dorn said flatly. "I found it over at the house where the kidnappers had taken Ronny. He'd been injected with it. And now we want to know what this is all about."

She was obviously aghast. "You can't do this," she gasped.

But my dear, I just have."

She tried to struggle out from under the bedsheet but Dorn shook his head and said, "I could restrain you, of course, until the Scop takes effect in about five minutes, but I would dislike to do it. Nor would there be much good in shouting for help. Barbara is the only other person in the house. And, besides, I could even gag you."

"You . . . you . . ."

He beamed at her. "Yes, my dear."

The two men sat and looked at her silently for several minutes. Her eyes began to glaze slightly.

Ronny said at last. "Did you give me those knockout drops?"

There was desperation behind her eyes, even in spite of the truth serum, but there was no possible escape.

"Yes," she said.

"Why?"

"So . . . that . . . my . . . accomplices . . . could . . . come . . . and . . . get . . . you."

"Told you so," Boy said. He was seated on the floor, his tongue hanging out, and still panting a bit from his exertions while guarding the return.

"Why did you want the location of the Dawnworlds?"

"So . . . that . . . we . . . could . . . go . . . there . . . and . . . learn . . . the . . . secret . . . of . . . the . . . elixir . . . of . . . life . . . the . . . prolonging . . . of . . . life . . . indefinitely . . . and . . . other . . . discoveries . . . they . . . have . . . made . . . such . . . as . . . the . . . matter . . . converter."

Both Ronny and Dorn were watching her in horror.

"You *fools*," Dorn snapped. "Would you run the chance of bringing destruction to the whole human race?"

130

"No."

"But how did you expect to get these secrets of theirs without antagonizing them? They destroy thieves, and even the sun systems from which the thieves come."

"We . . . did . . . not . . . plan . . . to . . . steal . . . anything. We . . . are . . . more . . . intelligent . . . than . . . they . . . are. We . . . planned . . . to . . . reason . . . them . . . into . . . freely . . . granting . . . us . . . the . . . discoveries."

"I can see you don't know, or understand, the Dawnmen," Ronny said with bitterness.

Dorn was looking at her contemplatively. He said, "Were all of the committee in on this?"

"No."

"Who was in on it besides you?"

"Barbara . . . and . . . Marvin."

"They are the committee members who arranged making you our guide and hostess?"

"Yes."

Ronny looked at the big man and chuckled. "So. It wasn't your overwhelming masculine charm that got Barbara into your bed. She wanted to distract you so that you wouldn't be around.

Dorn grunted at him. "Look who's talking. You didn't exactly sweep our girl, here, off her feet either. She was setting you up as a patsy." He turned back to Rosemary and said, "Why did you wish to gain admission into the United Planets?"

"Because . . . as . . . a . . . member . . . planet . . . we . . . would . . . come . . . under . . . Articles . . . One . . . and . . . Two . . . and . . . United . . . Planets . . . would . . . not . . . be . . . able . . . to . . . interfere . . . with . . .

131

our . . . plans . . . on . . . the . . . Dawnworlds. Otherwise . . . your . . . Space . . . Forces . . . might . . . have . . . interfered."

Ronny looked unbelieving. "But how did you expect to get away with kidnapping me? Obviously, when that came out, you'd have no chance of gaining entry to UP."

"We . . . didn't . . . plan . . . for . . . it . . . to . . . come . . . out. You . . . were . . . to . . .be . . . memory . . . washed . . . and . . . then . . . returned . . . here . . . to . . . me . . . in . . . bed. In . . . the . . . morning . . . when . . . we . . . both . . . awakened . . . you . . . would . . . not . . . remember . . . that . . . you . . . had . . . been . . . abducted . . . and . . . revealed . . . the . . . location . . . of . . . the . . . Dawnworlds."

Ronny was scowling at her in puzzlement. "But how could you possibly know that of all the Section G agents, Ross Metaxa would send me to Einstein?"

"We . . . guessed . . . he . . . would . . . send . . . agents . . . who . . . ranked . . . highest . . . in . . . intelligence. So . . . we . . . infiltrated . . . a . . . man . . . into . . . a . . . job . . . in . . . the . . . Interplanetary . . . Data . . . Banks . . . on . . . Earth . . . to . . . change . . . the . . . records . . . so . . . that . . . you . . . would . . . appear . . . to . . . be . . . highest . . . or . . . second . . . highest. The . . . plan . . . worked . . . out."

Dorn laughed and Ronny looked over at him in disgust. "What's so funny?"

"You're not as smart as you thought you were."

Ronny turned and headed for the door, saying, "We'd better report to Metaxa. This is bad."

Dorn said, "He's in London at some conference, but Sid Jakes is on hand." He looked down at the girl. "What about her?"

"What about her?" Ronny said disgustedly. "There's nothing further we can do with her. The Scop'll wear off in an hour or so. And we'd best let her do something about her chum-pals over at the other house. We don't want a killing on our hands on Einstein and, if I know you, some of those characters you creamed probably have at least a concussion."

He led the way out into the patio and headed toward the living room, Boy bringing up the rear. But at that point Fredric and Darlene came through the entry. On seeing the two Section G agents, both smiled and said good morning.

Ronny grunted his opinion of that and led the way to the living room.

Dorn went into the dining room for coffee while Ronny told the story to the two committee members.

When he was through, Fredric groaned and, seated now, put his head in his hands.

"You know nothing about this?" Ronny said, though he had already been told by Rosemary under Scop that none of the committee were involved save Marvin and Barbara.

Fredric shook his head. "It's well known that there is an element on Einstein that wants to secure the secrets of the Dawnworlds, especially their method of prolonging life indefinitely. In fact, I wouldn't mind knowing myself. Extending life for however long one would wish is a dream held by almost everyone."

"Then why weren't you in with them?"

Fredric looked up at him and said, "For the same reason that the majority of our people here on Einstein are not with them. We don't think they have a feasible plan to get the Dawnmen to release their

133

secrets. And we don't want to see Einstein wake up one morning with a methane-ammonia-hydrogen atmosphere."

Ronny said, "Well, now that they've been discovered, they can't be allowed to go to the Dawnworlds. They've got to be stopped."

Dorn came back with coffee and handed it around.

But Fredric and Darlene were staring at Ronny as though he had gone drivel-happy.

Darlene said very reasonably, "But there is no way of stopping them."

Ronny scowled at her. "What do you mean? Fredric just said that the majority of the population of Einstein is against the attempt."

Fredric put in, his voice equally reasonable, "But we have no means of coercion on Einstein."

Ronny closed his eyes in momentary mute appeal to higher powers. He said to Dorn, "Holy Ultimate, get Sid Jakes on the communicator."

He went over to the room's desk and plunked himself down in despair.

Boy, who was stretched out on the floor, his muzzle on crossed paws, said, "Fouled up mess, eh Boss?"

"You have said it." He looked down at the dog. "By the way, thanks for coming to the rescue."

The Vizsla gave his stubby tail a quick couple of wags, but said, "All part of the job, Boss. I'd offer to bite Marvin for you when he comes in, but I'm conditioned not to bite anybody on this planet."

Dorn brought his communicator over and propped it before Ronny. He said, his face unhappy, "You know, Ronny, we could go back to that other house and knock those four funkers off."

Fredric winced.

Ronny shook his head. "No, the word is spread by now. Besides, they're probably not even still there. They will have summoned a car and taken off."

Irene Kasansky's face faded in on the screen and immediately took on an expression of relief. "Ronny!" she said. "You're free!"

"Yeah," he said glumly. "Put Sid on, will you, Irene? You can listen in, if you want, and get the whole sad story."

"Will do."

The face of the assistant to Ross Metaxa faded in, grinning as usual. "Free already, eh? That was a neat trick. What happened?"

Dorn Horsten and Boy found me—too late."

"Who's Boy?"

"The latest member of the Section G team."

"Recruited a new potential agent, eh? Wizard. But what do you mean, too late?"

"They put me under Scop and dug the location of the Dawnworlds out of me."

Sid Jakes hissed, his expression less happy now. "Holy Ultimate! But why'd they want it? As though I didn't know."

"They're particularly interested in the prolongation of life. They wanted to get into UP so that Articles One and Two would apply to them and we wouldn't be able to stand in the way. Sid, they'll be heading for the Dawnworlds soonest, to get their business over before we can interfere."

"Yeah." Sid Jakes said, thinking about it. "It'd take a long time to get a Space Forces cruiser to you. Are there any spaceships available there?"

"There're two space freighters on the field. They look like tramps."

"Wizard. Hire one of them. Where would be a good planet to rendezvous with one of our cruisers? Some world partway there."

"New Delos or Xanadu."

"Just a minute." Sid Jakes turned his head and said something into an order-box. In a short time he came back to Ronny and said, "We have a medium class space cruiser within two days of New Delos. Meet them there and they'll take you to the Dawnworlds."

Ronny said, "Just a minute, Sid. If I give the officers of that space cruiser the coordinates of the Dawnworlds, then they'll know."

"We'll brainwash them later, like we did the men on the *Pisa*, who took you the first time."

"Wizard, but that was a four man scout. You're talking about a medium cruiser. And things worked out so that we could brainwash the *Pisa* crew. But suppose something falls apart on this expedition? The so-called Brahmins tolerated me on that first set-down on their planet, but they didn't suggest that they wanted me back. Anything could happen."

"I see what you mean," Jakes chuckled. "All right, let's do it this way. We'll send Lee Chang in a small cruiser from here. She'll get to New Delos as soon as you will. She's a navigator. She'll take over the navigating once you tell her where the Dawnworlds are, and the cruiser's officers won't know."

Ronny said cautiously, "What happens to Lee Chang after the whole romp is over, assuming we pull it off satisfactorily? Then *she'll* know where the Dawnworlds are."

Sid Jakes grinned at him. "We'll shoot her," he said. "And maybe you too."

15

Hiring the space freighter was no problem. As Ronny had suspected, one of them, the Space Freighter *Cherokee*, was a tramp and the skipper had no regular run. He would pick up a cargo on one planet, freight it to its destination and pick up a new load there for whatever spaceport it was designated for. He asked for an astronomical figure in interplanetary credits to take Ronny and Dorn to New Delos, his freighter going empty, since there was no cargo on Einstein for the world which had originally been settled by religious fanatics. Ronny shrugged that off. He was acting under orders. Let Sid Jakes worry about price.

However, the hope to New Delos was a lengthy one and the captain of the *Cherokee* found it necessary to take on additional fuel before getting under way.

The two Section G agents were climbing the walls with the need to get going, but there was nothing for it. The following morning was the soonest they could blast off. They returned to Rosemary's house.

The balance of the committee had shown up but Rosemary herself had flown the coop, and no one knew where she had gone.

Ronny and Dorn had eyed Marvin and Barbara in disgust.

Ronny said, "After what Academician Felix

Fitzjames told you about the dangers of the Deathworlds, you're still foolish enough to make an attempt on them?"

Marvin said stubbornly, "We're going to *request* that they release some of their technology to us, not try to seize it by force or steal it. We'll offer to exchange some of ours for theirs."

Ronny snorted and plunked down into a chair. "After a few megayears of their developing their science and technology, as compared to a couple of thousand years on the part of the human race, just what is it that you think that you've got that they'd want?"

Barbara said, "We don't know. But we are sending four of the most intelligent persons on Einstein. It will be a matter of consulting with the Dawnmen. From what Academician Fitzjames said, there is no difficulty whatsoever in communicating with them."

"No, there isn't," Ronny admitted. "They do it telepathically. Language makes no difference. But they do not like intruders."

He turned to Fredric. "Isn't there any possible way to stop them? Can't you put it to a vote, or something?"

Marvin said, "It's too late, anyway. They're on their way, and in the speediest spacecraft on Einstein." There was triumph in his voice.

"Holy Ultimate," Dorn said in disgust. "And we've got to wait until morning even to start."

In the morning, Fredric came down to the spaceport to see them off. He had another Vizsla with him. A female.

Boy said to her, "Hi, Puppy."

138

And she said scornfully, "The name is Plotz, as you very well know."

The whole group was walking toward the *Cherokee* from where they had parked the overcar which had brought them to the spaceport.

"Plotz?" Ronny said to Fredric.

"I dabble in writing," Fredric admitted ruefully. "What's wrong with Plotz as a name for a writer's dog? As she grows older, Plotz thickens."

"Oh, no," Dorn protested. "Don't tell me that with all the upgrading of intelligence on the planet Einstein, you still have the pun."

"She's a beautiful dog," Ronny made the mistake of saying, as they reached the space freighter's gangplank.

"Thank you," Plotz said, casting her eyes down demurely.

"She's yours," Fredric said immediately.

"Oh, now, see here..."

"No, really. It's better that you have a pair to take back with you to Earth. They breed true, you know. That is, the puppies, too, will talk and have superior intelligences."

Boy let his tongue hang out from the side of his mouth and gave a double pant as he eyed Plotz.

"Huh," she said.

Ronny looked at Fredric and said, "All right. Thanks. Earth will appreciate it. But listen, how do you people stand now on entry into United Planets? I know that Rosemary and her gang had ulterior motives for wishing to join, but how about the majority of you?"

"The majority of us still wish to join. Since we've found out about the presence of other intelligent life in the galaxy, we realize that man must stick together. It's not a matter of upgrading a single world, such as Einstein; the job must be to upgrade the whole race. We are willing to contribute our efforts to the common cause."

"Wizard," Ronny said. "We'll so report to our superiors. I don't know how they'll react, in view of this Dawnworlds foul-up, but I, personally, have no doubts about your own sincerity."

Fredric shook hands with the two Section G agents and they ascended the gangplank, followed by the two dogs, Plotz going first, lady that she was.

As she climbed the stair, Boy gave her rear end a quick sniff and she looked over her shoulder at him and said nastily, "If you don't look out you're going to get a nip."

"I didn't do anything," Boy said in defense, giving her a wag in reassurance.

Captain Joe Wald stood at the top of the gangplank awaiting his passengers. He looked down at the dogs for a long empty moment, then looked up accusingly at Ronny. "They talked," he said.

"Yeah," Ronny said. "Everything's brainy on this world."

When Boy came abreast the skipper, he stuck up his paw to be shaken and said, "Glad to be aboard, Captain. My name's Boy."

Wald, looking as blank as had Ronny and Dorn when they had first come in contact with the talking dog, first shook his head, then shook the paw.

The skipper led the way to their quarters, which were ample enough. In her day, before becoming a tramp, the *Cherokee* had been an interplanetary passenger-freighter with accommodations for twenty, in addition to the crew. She seldom carried passengers these days, being on the rundown side, but the cabins were still available.

The run to New Delos was uneventful and Ronny and Dorn killed most of the time either reading or playing battle chess. Spotted two tanks and a machine gun nest, Ronny sometimes even won.

Largely, they avoided discussing their mission. There was simply nothing more to say at this point.

An exception was one day, after they had wearied of playing, when out of a clear sky Ronny exploded.

"Those damn Einstein funkers," he snarled.

Dorn looked over at him.

Ronny said, "The bastards supposedly have the best brains mankind has ever developed and look at what they're doing. Risking the whole race."

Dorn thought about it. "It was you," he said mildly, "who pointed out that high intelligence doesn't guarantee integrity."

He pushed his glasses back on the bridge of his nose and went on. "In developing a viable intelligent life form, you have three requirements, a brain, a hand with an opposed thumb, or its equivalent, and a voice box with its necessary complement, the ear—or the equivalent, such as telepathy. Once given those basics, you can begin to develop all three. In a surprisingly short time, speaking in terms of evolution of species, the brain can be augmented. Bringing the hand up from the point where it can grasp and utilize a sharp rock to where it can thread a needle or assemble a micro-computer, is also possible. Evolving the voice box from the point where it can grunt, bark and whine to the level where it can render the Jewel Song from *Faust*, and evolving an ear that will appreciate the effort, is time-consuming, but it only takes time.

"But the evolution of a high ethic is still more time-consuming and man, certainly, is still at the task. The sands of our beaches are littered with those who have drowned in the attempt, from the Hebrew prophets, through the Buddah and Joshua of Nazareth to more recent examples, some too close to us for us to realize that this was what they were attempting to do. Our Voltaires, our Tom Paines, our Lincolns, our Ghandis, not to mention so many of our poets."

Ronny said, "Wizard. I've never heard you wax so poetic, Dorn."

Boy, who had been sprawled out on the floor next to Plotz, opened one eye and said, accusingly, "How's a dog supposed to get any sleep around here?"

They ignored him and Dorn said, "Evidently, our friends from Einstein have yet to achieve a high ethic. We can only hope that the Dawnmen are more advanced in this respect."

Ronny snorted deprecation at that. He said, "The planet Phrygia now has an atmosphere of methane, hydrogen and ammonia, as a result of the Dawnworlds' attack. Does that sound like a high ethical code?"

"They were provoked," Dorn said unhappily.

Ronny Bronston had been on New Delos once before. In fact, it had been the first planet, save Earth, he had ever set down upon. It had been his first assignment and Lee Chang Chu had been along to shepherd the fledging Section G agent. Theoretically, he had been in pursuit of the legendary

142

Tommy Paine, an interplanetary revolutionist who had participated in the overthrow of a score of governments, socioeconomic systems and even religions. His latest escapade had been assisting the local revolutionists in the assassination, with a bomb, of the immortal god-king of New Delos. The planet was governed by a very restrictive theocracy, headed by this god-king, who supposedly never died. In actuality, approximately every twenty years, the ruling bishops of the church would get together and elect from their number a new head. Plastic surgery would then be used so that the new god-king would look exactly like the old to the people. Reactionary though the government was, there had seldom been revolt. It takes a brave man to rebel against both his kind and his god. However, Tommy Paine supposedly entered onto the scene and the god-king, while being televised all over the planet, was assassinated by the local revolutionists. The revolution then took place overnight, and was in full swing when Ronny and Lee Chang had arrived.

It was only later that Ronny Bronston found out that there was no such person as Tommy Paine. He was, in actuality, a cover for Section G when they secretly committed some of their subversive acts against members of United Planets who were failing to progress because of reactionary institutions.

New Delos had changed considerably since Ronny had been there before. For one thing, the capital city, formerly on the sleepy side, had doubled in size and was abustle with activity. The spaceport was also considerably larger and there were a dozen spaceships of varying size on the field. Obviously, New Delos was conducting a wide trade with her fellow members of United Planets. Under the god-kind she had been what amounted to a hermit planet, with as little intercourse with other worlds as she could manage.

Among the spaceships, was a Space Forces cruiser. Captain Joe Wald set the *Cherokee* down as near to it as he could.

Ronny Bronston and Dorn Horsten had long since packed. They said hurried goodbyes and, accompanied by the dogs, started in the direction of the SFC *Alexander Hamilton*.

Plotz, happy at the chance for some exercise after the cooped up period on the *Cherokee* trotted ahead.

Ronny looked down at Boy, who was pacing along beside him. He said, "What are you looking so smug about?"

Boy hung his tongue out for a couple of quick pants and said, "Didn't you notice? Plotz was in heat, back on the *Cherokee*."

Ronny rolled his eyes upward. "Oh, wizard. A great lover I've got on my hands. She'll probably have the pups before we get back to Earth—always assuming we do."

Boy gave his bobbed tail several wags. "Sixty-three days," he said with satisfaction. "Gestation period is about sixty-three days. I understand that you humans take nine months. Waste of time."

Lee Chang Chu and a tall, uniformed Space Forces officer were awaiting them at the top of the gangplank. As always, she was dressed in a silken *Cheongsam*. And, just as characteristic, she was demurely smiling as the two Section G agents approached, a mere Oriental woman in the presence of men.

144

When Ronny and Dorn reached the hatchway she said, "Supervisor Ronald Bronston, Agent Dorn Horsten, let me introduce you to Captain John Fodor, commander of the Cruiser *Alexander Hamilton*."

The three men shook hands. The captain was, tall, sparce, about forty and gave the impression of being the no-nonsense type. He radiated the air of spaceman.

Lee Chang looked down at the dogs and said, "Where in the world did you acquire these two beautiful animals?"

Ronny said, "Lee Chang, meet Boy and Plotz."

Boy stuck out his paw for a shake and said, "Hello. You the Boss' female?"

Lee Chang's almond eyes widened and her chin dropped a little. She shook the offered paw, and darted a quick look up at Ronny.

She said, "Why, no. Why do you ask?"

"It's the way you two look at each other," he told her. "Meet my bitch friend."

Plotz extended a paw and said, "I am happy to meet you, Lee Chang."

The captain was gaping too.

Ronny said to him, "Let's get spaceborne soonest, skipper. We're in the biggest hurry, ever."

"Where are we bound for?" Captain Fodor said.

"We'll tell you later. For the time, set a course in the direction of Xanadu."

"Right," the captain said. He looked down at the dogs again, shook his head, then turned and headed toward the cruiser's bridge, saying over his shoulder, "Supervisor Lee Chang Chu will show you to your quarters."

Carrying the bags, the two agents followed her, the dogs bringing up the rear.

She said, "You have the second officer's cabin. He's doubling up with the third deck officer. I'm right next to you in the first officer's quarters. He's moved in with the first engineer."

The door to their new quarters was open and they found the cabin on the Spartan side, but comfortable. Somebody had improvised a second bunk and Dorn was pleased to see that it was ample in size for his bulk. Evidently, Lee Chang had given them the word on his size.

While the men were putting their bags down, Lee Chang put her hands on her hips and said, "Ronny Bronston, have you been studying ventriloquism? I couldn't even catch your mouth moving."

He grinned at her. "Nope," he said. "They really talk. In fact, I sometimes think Boy talks too damn much."

"Some nerve," Boy said, but he gave his stub of a tail a double wag to indicate he wasn't really upset at the charge.

Dorn said, "They come from Einstein and on that planet they not only upbreed themselves with a vengeance but evidently everything else."

Ronny said to the Chinese operative, "This cruiser is bigger than I expected."

"It was the only one immediately available," Lee Chang told him.

"How big's the crew?"

"The captain and three deck officers. The chief engineer and three engineer officers. And a chief steward. That's the officers. There are thirty in the crew, of varying ranks."

146

"Damn," Ronny said. "It's too many. The fewer people that see anything at all of the Dawnworlds, the better."

"I've thought about that," she said, nodding. "I think our best plan is to set-down and we three disembark and the cruiser blast-off again immediately and go into orbit, with instruction not to use the scanners to observe the surface. We'll keep in laser beam communication with them and call to come and get us, when required."

They could feel the spaceship tremble beneath them and knew that they were underway.

They found seats and for a moment looked at each other in silence.

"Who's in command, among the three of us?" Ronny said finally.

"You are," Lee Chang said. "We're both of supervisor rank, but you're in charge."

"You're my senior."

"But you've been on the Dawnworlds before. You're the only one who has—at least the only one who remembers."

He didn't argue. She made sense. As little as he really knew about the Dawnmen, it was more than anybody else did.

He said, "How's the *Alexander Hamilton* armed?"

"The same as all other cruisers of this class."

"Wizard. We'll have the skipper jettison all weapons. That includes everything, even our H-guns, if you brought them along."

Lee Chang and Dorn both eyed him questioningly.

Ronny said, "I don't want to approach that first

147

Dawnworld we'll come to with as much in the way of a potentially deadly article as a fly swatter, not to speak of laser weapons, nuclear weapons and such."

Lee Chang nodded. "I suppose you're right. We want to give every indication of friendly, peaceful intent."

They met most of the balance of the cruiser's officers in the mess at the noon meal. Except for the first officer and the first engineer, both of whom were on watch, the full complement were on hand. Lee Chang, who had come with them from Earth, was already well known, and, as usual, it was obvious that, to a man, they were in love with the provocative Chinese. She introduced them all and then made the ship's officers acquainted with the two dogs. Boy went around wagging and offering his right front paw to each in turn.

"Hi," he'd say. "Glad to meet you."

Plotz had simply said, "It's a pleasure to make your acquaintance," wagged her tail a few times, to guarantee the truth of her statement and remained in the background.

Except for one muttered, "I don't believe it," the Space Forces men simply ogled.

The captain said, "All right, all right. Let us get down to the nitty-gritty." He looked at Ronny. "Citizen Lee Chang Chu has been most secretive. She would tell us nothing about our destination, saying that we'd have to wait until our rendezvous with you and Doctor Horsten."

Lee Chang said quietly, "In actuality, I don't even know it, Captain."

Ronny put his fork down and said simply, "Our destination is unknown, Captain. What exactly were the orders that you were given?"

The captain was staring at him. "To put my ship and my crew under your orders and to carry out your every order—to the death, if necessary. They were issued to me by the President of United Planets himself. What do you mean, you don't know our destination, Supervisor Bronston?"

"I didn't mean that. When I said our destination is unknown, I meant that it will remain unknown to you, your officers and the crew. I am the only person that knows it. And shortly Supervisor Chu will. You will never know where you have gone or where you have been."

The skipper was looking at him as though he had gone completely around the bend. So were his officers.

Captain Fodor said, "My dear sir, how am I going to be able to take you to this mysterious destination if I don't know where it is?"

"Who is your navigator?"

"Traditionally, the second deck officer is navigator. Mr. Tokugawa, here. But the captain also double checks the navigating and, if needed, overrules the second officer."

Very well," Ronny told him. "And who is in charge of the star charts?"

"Mr. Tokugawa and myself."

"Wizard. Supervisor Lee Chang Chu is also a spaceship navigator. I will reveal the coordinates of our destination to her. She will do the navigating. During our journey, even while in under-space, Mr. Tokugawa will not be allowed on the bridge at any time. And you, yourself, will not be allowed on it while Lee Chang is setting our courses."

The captain's face went indignant. He said stiffly, "This is my ship, sir."

"And you are under the direct orders of the President of United Planets."`

Captain Fodor glared at him for a long moment. Finally, "Very well, sir."

Lee Chang said quietly, "I think it would be best if all star charts would be placed in my custody, in my stateroom, and that a guard be placed at the door on a twenty-four hour a day basis."

"What in the hell's going on!" the captain demanded in indignation.

Dorn Horsten spoke up for the first time in his quiet voice. "The fate of the human race is going on," he said.

"Dogs too, evidently," Boy murmured.

After the meal, for the next few hours in their own quarters, the five of them rehashed the developments on Einstein, Lee Chang being only partially acquainted with them. Ronny pulled no punches, admitting that he had been suckered by Rosemary, giving her the opportunity to drug him, and leading to his being given Scop and his mind being picked.

She said, her soft voice gently mocking, "I didn't know that you were that susceptible to feminine charms, Ronny."

He looked at her in irritation. "I'm a man, damn it."

"On the face of it," she nodded sweetly.

She thought about it for a moment, then said, "I suppose that the quicker you give me the coordinates of the Dawnworlds, the sooner I can get to setting as direct a course as possible for the nearest one."

"Yes, certainly," Ronny said. He looked at Dorn apologetically. "I think that it's better that not even you be in on it."

The doctor pushed his glasses back on the bridge of his nose and said emphatically, "I most certainly agree with you. What I do not know, I cannot betray, even under Scop. I have sometimes wondered, in reflection, whether or not Ross Metaxa shouldn't have brainwashed you as well as the crew of the *Pisa* and Rita Daniels. Possibly *nobody* should know the location of the Dawnworlds. You say that they are in an obscure spiral, off the beaten track, and that ordinarily we wouldn't stumble upon them for ages. Very well, just knowing that they are out there, somewhere, is enough, that and the information we have about them. Sooner or later, stumble upon them we will—and the later the better."

"We'll leave you here with the dogs," Ronny said. "Obviously, they, too, can't hear what I have to tell Lee Chang."

Don't you trust me, Boss?" Boy said, giving a quick double pant and obviously just kidding. The super-pooch even had a sense of humor.

"Shut up," Ronny said, escorting Lee Chang toward the door and toward her own quarters.

He closed and locked the door behind him.

"Why, Ronny," she said modestly.

He grunted at her and looked at the door. "I imagine that's sound proof and proof everything else, for that matter. But I wonder if there's the chance of an icicle in hell that this cabin could be bugged."

"No," she said. "Sid Jakes had a team of our people go through the *Alexander Hamilton* like a fine comb. A cockroach couldn't be on it that we didn't know about. And each crewman and officer was searched down to the last mote of dust in his clothes, before coming aboard. There's no bug in this cabin—or anywhere else on the cruiser."

"Wizard," he said. "All right, these are the coordinates of the Dawnworlds. To be exact, the coordinates of the one I first landed upon. The same coordinates those Einstein cloddies have."

He gave them to her and she mentally noted them down, rather than risking any written record.

She nodded and said, "Very well. We're already headed in the general direction. Tomorrow, I'll take over the bridge and drop us into under-space, after taking every star chart they have. I'd have to look at a chart, but from memory I think you're probably correct. They're located in such a spiral that I doubt that, ordinarily, we would have come in contact for some time."

He came to his feet, saying, "I suppose I should get back to Dorn and the dogs."

She stood, too, and the sides of her mouth turned down. "But, Ronny," she said. "You said you were a man—damn it, as you put it. And here we are. You have me in a locked room."

He gaped at her. "What is that supposed to mean?"

Her almond eyes took him in, in amusement. "Don't you think that you'd be more comfortable in here with me than with Dorn and the dogs?"

She turned and looked at the bunk. "There seems to be room for the two of us. After all these years, Ronny, you've still never approached me."

"I . . . I didn't know that you were available."

"You never asked," she said, a slightly mocking element in her voice.

152

16

The hop from New Delos to the first Dawnworld planet was as uneventful as that from Einstein to New Delos had been, though longer.

On the second day Lee Chang confiscated all star charts and put them under lock and key in her cabin. The captain had looked miffed, but said nothing. All of them, of course, were not required but if she had allowed some to remain in the chart room they would have been a clue to where the Dawnworlds were not.

She and Ronny went to the bridge and politely requested that all ship's personnel currently on watch retire. They looked at Captain Fodor.

He said, "We are under the command of these representatives of the Bureau of Investigation of the Department of Justice, of the Commissariat of Interplanetary Affairs. Their orders override my own, even though I am commander of this cruiser."

The spacemen marched out and Lee Chang took her place at the controls.

She said, "Just as a double check, give me those coordinates again. I remember them, but just to be sure."

He gave them to her.

She looked it up on the star chart before her and nodded. "Mapped only by radio telescope. No indication that human manned exploration ships have ever touched there."

She set a course and then came out of her chair, folding her star chart.

"That's it, Ronny," she said. "Let's get this back to my cabin and under lock."

Ronny spent the rest of the hop staying in Lee Chang's cabin at nights. Whether or not the cruiser's officers were aware of this he didn't know. However, by the envious expressions he sometimes caught on their faces he suspected that they did. He couldn't have cared less.

The hours that they could have together with each other were precious. He had told her the truth. They were expendable and it was unlikely that they would ever return from this assignment. There was, almost without doubt, no future for their relationship.

The difficulty was that it was becoming increasingly close. He mentally kicked himself for not having established it sooner. He had never suspected that the beautiful Chinese had been attracted to him. Every unmarried agent in Section G was head over heels for Lee Chang and Ronny had no illusions about his own masculine charms. He had always been on the unprepossessing side in appearance.

When they came out of underspace, it was in the vicinity of the Dawnman planet where Baron Wyler, later followed by Ronny and agent Phil Birdman, had originally set-down.

They held a conference with the captain on the bridge.

Ronny said, "Somewhere on the planet below is probably an Earth-type spacecraft. At least, I assume that they got here first. You can detect it?"

"Of course."

"Very well. Please locate it and set down in its

154

vicinity. Supervisor Lee Chang Chu, Doctor Horsten and myself will disembark. To the extent possible, you will prevent your officers and crew seeing anything whatsoever of the surface of this planet. I know you can't accomplish this completely, but to the extent possible."

The captain sighed in exasperation.

Ronny went on. "As soon as we are disembarked, you will lift off again and go into orbit, a high enough orbit that you will be unable to observe details of the surface of this world. We will communicate with you at least once every six hours. If a period goes by in which we do not do so, you are immediately to attempt to return to Earth where you will report to my superiors, in Section G of the Bureau of Investigation, that the mission has proved a failure and that I recommend a mobilization of the Space Forces, as hopeless as that might be."

"What do you mean, I'll *attempt* to return to Earth?" Captain Fodor said.

"He means just that," Dorn said flatly.

The captain said, in irritation, "How can I get back to Earth if I don't even know where I am? To navigate in underspace you've got to know the coordinates of where you start from as well as those of where you are going."

Lee Chang Chu said softly, "I have left a star chart on the table in my cabin. It is sealed. On it is marked our present location. If we fail to communicate with you, break the seal and attempt to return to Earth."

"If you make it, you'll probably be memory washed," Ronny said. "Reveal this location to nobody, not even your navigator. Do the navigating yourself. There has never been a top secret more top secret than this in the history of the human race, Captain."

Captain Fodor looked at him. "I wish the hell I knew what was going on," he growled.

And Ronny looked back at him emptily. "So do I," he said. "Let's get this show on the road."

With only his first officer on the bridge, and the three Section G agents, Captain Fodor set about locating the spaceship from Einstein. They went into orbit, the *Alexander Hamilton's* sensors scanning the planet below.

After a time, the captain scowled and said, "This world is unpopulated. There's not a sign of cities or even towns. There's no sign, even, of individual buildings, houses or whatever. There are no ships on the seas."

Ronny sighed and said, "It's not unpopulated, Captain. However, the less I tell you about it, the better."

The first officer, as mystified as his commanding officer, was at the sensors, the captain sitting before a viewing screen at the space cruiser's controls.

John Fodor said to Ronny, "After I put you down, and go into orbit, as you directed, what shall I do if I am intercepted by elements of their spacefleet? I assume they have a spacefleet."

"Yes," Ronny said grimly. "They have one. I suggest that you might try prayer."

The captain eyed him disgustedly but went back to his controls.

They finally spotted the spaceship from Einstein on the side of the Dawnworld almost directly opposite to where Ronny Bronston had landed before.

Ronny said to the captain, "All right. Set down

156

about half a kilometer from them, preferably behind a hill. For all I know the cloddies may have weapons and might take a shot at us."

The captain set down with care and immediately activated the hatchway, after questioning Ronny about the need for spacesuits. The Section G agent had shaken his head. The atmosphere was almost identical to that which prevailed on humanity settled worlds, as was the gravity.

John Fodor saw the three to the gangplank and watched after them.

Boy, who had been tagging along, with Plotz behind him, said, "Do we come, Boss?"

Ronny looked down at him. "Why?"

Boy gave a double pant. "You never know. Maybe you'll have occasion to trail somebody, or scout on ahead, or something. We're Vizslas, best trailers anywhere."

"All right. Come along."

Boy gave him a triple wag of his bobbed tail and started down the gangplank after Lee Chang, Dorn and his master. Plotz brought up the rear.

The captain called after them, "Good luck."

As soon as they had cleared out of the immediate vicinity, the *Alexander Hamilton* took off again, as ordered.

The three looked about. Save for the differences in flora, the Dawnworld looked remarkably like Einstein. It seemed to be one great park. For that matter, the plant life had developed as it had on many of the Earth-settled worlds. Dorn Horsten decided inwardly that given the same type of atmosphere, the same gravity, that it wasn't too surprising.

Ronny said, "This way, isn't it?" and headed off in

the direction of the Einstein spaceship. The two dogs ranged ahead, as though trying to flush birds.

Ronny put his right hand out before him and said, "Now this is the way you walk on a Dawnworld."

Both Lee Chang and Dorn stared at him.

"Why?" Dorn said.

"So you won't run into a house and smash your nose."

Lee Chang said, worry in her voice, "Ronny, what's wrong with you?"

He came to a halt for a moment to explain to them. "The captain was wrong when he said there were no buildings down here. The Dawnmen are something like the people of Einstein. They don't like the landscape to be cluttered up with buildings. On Einstein they solve the problem by putting all buildings underground. On the Dawnworlds they make them invisible."

"Invisible?" Lee Chang said in puzzlement.

"Yes. Invisible and transparent. You can walk right into one. You can feel the wall, but you can't see it whatsoever. Evidently, the Dawnmen can, somehow, but we can't."

They took his word for it and each of them extended a hand before him as they walked.

They came upon no houses or other buildings between the point where they had set down and the Einstein spaceship.

Arrived at their destination, they stared up at it. It was a small passenger craft. Ronny suspected that it was one of the spaceships the scientists of Einstein utilized from time to time to journey to conferences held on other worlds.

158

The hatchway was open, the gangplank was out, but there was no one.

"Hallo!" Dorn called out.

There was no response.

Boy looked up at Ronny and said, "Want me to take a look, Boss?"

Ronny said, "Yes."

The dog was up the gangplank in a trice and had disappeared into the ship's bowels. The three Section G agents and Plotz waited.

Finally, Boy emerged and looked down at them. "Nobody aboard, Boss," he said.

Ronny leading, the three agents mounted the gangplank and entered.

The craft was well outfitted, something like a space yacht. It would, undoubtedly, have accommodated at least a double dozen of passengers, plus a crew. They went from cabin to cabin, double-checking on Boy, and found that only five of the cabins had been occupied and, by the looks of them, by four men and one woman.

They wound up in the spaceship's lounge and sank into seats. The two dogs settled to the floor.

"What now?" Dorn said. "Where do you think they might be?"

"Damned if I know," Ronny growled. "If they tried any tricks they might already be dead. When I was here last, the Dawnmen had a small complex of very ancient buildings, that looked as though they were of religious nature, temples and pyramids. On top of the largest pyramid was an altar. I didn't see it in use, but the captain of the *Pisa* and Baron Wyler and Fitzjames did. The Dawnmen used an obsidian

159

knife to open the chest cavity of the victims so they could pull out the heart. The whole crew of Wyler's yacht went that way."

"Good heavens," Lee Chang said in feminine protest.

Dorn was scowling at Ronny. He said, "Do they do that to all strangers?"

"No. They didn't do it to me, nor Wyler and Fitzjames. Wyler's crew had attempted to purloin some of the Dawnman devices. But they warned us to leave. There is nothing in the rituals by which they live to provide for intercourse with strangers."

And at that moment a voice entered into the mind of each of them.

You are correct, Ronald Bronston; there is no place in our society for the stranger. We warned you not to return to our worlds and to warn off your race. But instead, you have come again and, through your informing others of our location, they came as well.

Ronny said, in protest, "I came, with my friends here, only to warn the others away, to prevent them from antagonizing you."

Nevertheless, you came, and must bear the consequences. As must the others. They attempted, in their arrogance, to confound us, to rob us of discoveries we made aeons past. But we are aware that if we released our technology to other life forms they would then be in a position to confront us and, possibly, one day to destroy us. Now, they cannot, for our technology is the most advanced of which we know in the whole galaxy.

Beyond that, neither your home planets, nor that of these other strangers, are ready for the advances

160

which we have made long since. If you were, you would have developed them yourselves. Let me dip into your minds for an example in your own history. You had a primitive early man in the early millenea of your race. The Neanderthal. Would you have turned over to a Neanderthal a highly powered, internal combustion vehicle of the type which I can discern in your minds, and taught him to drive it? Had you, he most likely would have killed someone, and probably himself.

Dorn Horsten said, "What do you plan to do with us?"

It is now out of the hands of we whom you once called the Brahmins of the Dawnworlds. To carry on the similes of your Academician Count Felix Fitzjames, there are three ancient castes on our worlds, the Brahmins, whom I represent, the Kshatriyas, who were originally our ruling class and warriors, and the Sudras, the working class. It was long ago that these castes were formed, long, long ago, but still we keep our ancient traditions.

"What do you mean, it's out of your hands, out of the hands of you Brahmins?" Lee Chang wavered.

You will be turned over to the Kshatriyas for their annual ceremonies.

17

"What annual ceremonies?" Ronny demanded.

But suddenly all three realized that the intelligence that had been communicating with them telepathically had withdrawn. They stared at each other, aghast.

Through all this, the two dogs had been stretched out on the floor, Boy growling low in his throat, all but inaudibly. Now he said, "What was all that, Boss? I seemed to be hearing somebody talking—in my head."

"Me too," Plotz said, a worried whine in her voice.

"We all heard it," Ronny told them. "They can evidently communicate, no matter what the language, with any intelligent life form."

"What do we do now?" Dorn said.

"What can we do?" Ronny said. "All we can do is wait and see what happens."

Lee Chang said, not very convincingly, "I could probably pilot this spacecraft. We could take off and rejoin the *Alexander Hamilton*."

"No," Ronny told her. "I doubt if they'd let us. Besides, our mission isn't finished. Somehow, we've got to keep them from sending out their fleet to polish off United Planets."

He took his communicator from his pocket, activated it and said into the screen, "Ronald

Bronston, calling Captain John Fodor of the Space Forces Cruiser *Alexander Hamilton.*"

The captain's face faded in immediately. "Supervisor Bronston," he said. "Are you all right?"

"We're still alive," Ronny said laconically. "We've made contact with the people we came to see. Are you okay, up there?"

"Yes. Everything is routine."

"Wizard. Carry on, then. We'll contact you, as arranged, within another six hours."

He switched off the communications device and thought about it for a minute, then switched it back on again and flicked a stud. "Ronald Bronston, calling Irene Kasansky" he said.

Irene's face faded in and when she saw who it was turned apprehensive. "Ronny," she said. "Are you three all right?"

"Well, so far we're still with it. Is the old man available?"

Ross Metaxa's face, tired and moist of eye as always, took the place of Irene's in the small screen. He looked at Ronny questioningly.

Ronny said, "It looks bad, sir. Briefly, the others got here first. We're in their ship. They're missing. We've been contacted by one of the, uh, Brahmins. It doesn't look as though they're going to let us go this time."

"What are their plans for United Planets?"

"I don't know."

"Should I recommend to the President that the Space Forces fleet be mobilized?"

"Certainly not yet. Not while we're still here and working on it. I told Fodor that if they did us in, he should recommend it, but it won't do any good. The last time I was here I saw one of their spacecraft. It was a hundred times the size of the largest spacecraft we've got. And it was even able to turn itself invisible. We're scheduled to be turned over to their soldier caste for something they call their annual ceremonies. It doesn't sound so good."

"All right, Ronny," his superior sighed wearily. "Do what you can." His face faded.

The three stared at each other some more without words. There was nothing to say.

Lee Chang said finally, "Should I check out the ship's galley? We could eat something before whatever comes next."

"I couldn't eat anything," Ronny said.

"I could," Boy said, giving the Chinese girl a couple of wags. "I can always eat something."

"Chowhound," Plotz said, with the nearest thing to a sneer she could put over, but she too got up to follow Lee Chang.

But it was then that a voice came into all of their minds. The Brahmin's had been calm, gentle, and in accord with the fact that he was a scholar. This voice had a ring of command.

You will leave the space vessel.

Ronny looked at Lee Chang and then Dorn and came to his feet. He said, "I doubt that disobeying would make much sense. Not to speak of physically resisting."

They stood, too, wordlessly, and followed him, the two dogs coming along behind.

Boy growled, "By the way, Boss, that conditioning of mine, not to bite people, applies only on Einstein."

Ronny said, "Well, don't try it."

164

At the top of the gangplank he looked out. Below were nine Dawnmen. Eight of them were drawn up in a squad, the other, obviously in command, was out in front. All were somewhat over six feet in height and all in the vicinity of one hundred and ninety pounds. All were golden of skin, dark cream of hair. They could have been brothers, so similar were they. Not exactly twins, but very similar, including the officer. All were clothed in identical shorts, nothing else, and all wore sandals. The eight bore what looked like Neptune's trident, of mythology. Their leader carried a swagger stick.

Ronny wasn't deluded. They might not look very efficiently armed, or dangerous, but he knew better. He started down the gangway and was followed by the others.

He marched up to the officer and said, "Okay. What do you want?"

The officer turned and looked at his men, without speaking. Evidently, he didn't have to speak. Four of them stepped forward briskly a few paces, then snappily executed a left face and started marching off.

Into the minds of the three Earthlings and their dogs came the order, *Follow*.

They fell in behind the four.

Behind them, they could hear the remaining four take their place in the march. The officer strode to one side.

Dorn said to Ronny, "Was this the way they dressed the last time you were here?"

"Yes."

"I get the impression that the climate is always the same. No seasons. Always perfect. They must have

165

unbelievably competent climatic engineers."

"They've got unbelievably competent every-thing," Ronny said sourly. "I wonder where in the hell we're being taken."

Boy, trotting along beside Ronny, had been sizing up the Dawnmen. He gave a couple of pants and said, "The way they dress, you could really get in a nifty bite on the calf of a leg."

"Shut up," Ronny said.

Into their minds came another message. *What kind of an . . . animal is that?*

Ronny wondered why the Dawnmen ever asked questions. If they could read his mind, and memory, they could find the answer to any question they might want to ask. Well, perhaps it was simpler, or faster, or whatever. Or possibly only the Brahmins could read memory.

He said, "It's a dog. On Earth and on most of the humanity-settled planets, we keep them as pets."

Pets?

It seemed that the Kshatriyas, even the officers, weren't as astute as the Brahmins. The Brahmin who had contacted them would have been able to dig out man's relationship to his pets with no difficulty. But then, that made sense. The Brahmins were the brains of the Dawnworlds, the Kshatriyas were the soldiers. The Dawnmen Ronny had seen on his first visit were Sudras and hadn't communicated with him at all; in fact, they hadn't even seemed aware of his existence.

He said, "They serve as companions to us and live in our homes with us. They guard our houses and sometimes have special tasks such as herding other animals."

Boy looked up at him and said, "Sure enough,

166

Boss. How about pulling dog sleds in Alaska in the old days, stuff like that? I read a book once by an Earth-side writer named Jack London."

That was the extent of the questioning. They marched on.

Their destination wasn't far. They had covered approximately a kilometer and a half when an order came into their minds.

Halt!

Simultaneously, the four Dawnmen before them came to a snappy halt and they could hear those behind do the same.

The officer strode forward and suddenly a door opened before him, seemingly in the clear air. Ronny had seen the astonishing phenomenon before but Lee Chang gasped and Dorn's eyes bugged. Beyond the door could be made out a furnished room.

Enter.

They filed through and the door closed behind them.

The surprise was in the lack of surprise. The room beyond was not as different as all that. In fact, Ronny Bronston couldn't help comparing it to those in the monasteries of the planet Saint Athos which had been settled by a Greek religious order. It was cell-like, and there was no decoration whatsoever—as befitted a bee-hive culture. The furniture looked comfortable and utilitarian. It came to the Section G agent than any humanoid life form would evolve much the same furniture, the chair, the table, the bed, the couch. But no. The table was off-beat. There were no legs to hold it up. The top just hung there in the air. Some form of anti-gravity was being used.

The other surprise came in the fact that Rosemary was seated on a couch. There was no one else in the room. It was obvious that it was a living room, and doors opened off two of the walls. At least, Ronny assumed they were doors; there were neither knobs nor locks.

Rosemary was staring at them. Then she started to her feet, saying, "Ronny! Dorn! You've come to our rescue!"

Dorn snorted at that and Ronny said bitterly, "Evidently, we've come to join you. Where are the others?"

"In the...I suppose you'd call it the dining room...eating. I wasn't hungry. I can't bear their food." She looked at Lee Chang, who had been taking her in.

Ronny said, "Rosemary, this is Supervisor Lee Chang Chu of the Bureau of Investigation. She and Dorn and I have been sent to attempt to prevent you from precipitating a crisis which would result in the destruction of United Planets and other Earth-settled worlds, including your own."

The two women nodded warily at each other. What is there about the eternal female? Ronny wondered inwardly.

Boy had wandered over to one of the windows, which looked out upon the park-like scenery. "Some house," he said.

Plotz settled down on the floor and promptly went to sleep, her nose on crossed paws.

Rosemary said, "I'll go and get the others."

But Ronny said, "There's no hurry. Let them finish their meal. Are there accommodations here for sleeping?"

"Yes, ample." The Einstein girl settled back wearily onto the couch, adding, "This amounts to a prison. There is no way of getting out."

Dorn turned and looked at the door through which they had entered.

She said, "There's no way of opening it."

The big man said thoughtfully, "Have you tried breaking it down?"

"If you even approach it, you get a crashing headache."

The three newcomers found seats and relaxed into them.

"Suppose you tell us your story," Lee Chang said. "You might have some information we haven't come upon as yet."

Rosemary said, "I doubt it. The story is simple enough. With the knowledge we secured from Ronny under Scop we immediately took off for this destination. We met with complete failure. We still believe we have superior minds to the, uh, Brahmins but we were utterly unable to get through their barriers of traditions and rituals. There is simply no place for intercourse with strangers in this culture. They're ... they're like ants. Everybody in his place, everybody to his task. The anthill is everything, the individual is nothing. All outsiders are enemies. Well, not exactly enemies, they're just ignored.

"Immediately upon our setting down, we were mentally contacted by ... by one of the Brahmins. We never saw him. He refused even to consider turning any of their technology over to us. He told us that we would not be allowed to leave, for fear we would inform others of the location of the Dawnworlds. We attempted to blast off and escape

169

but the controls of the spaceship wouldn't respond. Instead, we were turned over to the equivalent of soldier ants, I suppose you could call them, and brought here."

Dorn said, "You made no effort to resist?"

"Two of the men had guns but they wouldn't function. One of them attempted to physically assault one of the soldier ants and was paralyzed before he got to within six feet of him. The paralysis wore off in about five minutes but, obviously, he didn't try again. We were brought to this place."

Lee Chang said, "How long have you been here?"

"We don't know. Our devices measuring time are not operative. And there is no night and day here. It always seems to be high noon. But I would say, by the number of times we have eaten, that we've been here approximately a week."

One of the inner doors opened and two men entered, showing their surprise at seeing the newcomers. They were typical of those Ronny and Dorn had met on Einstein, and both looked as though they were somewhere in their early thirties.

Rosemary introduced all around. The two were Roy and David. No second names, in the Einstein fashion. Everyone had barely gotten beyond the point of shaking hands when the door opened again and two more entered the room. They were Charles and Gil.

All seated, Ronny took over. He said, looking about at the five representatives from Einstein, "We're all in the same spot. Our interests were, and are, different, but for the sake of survival the obvious need is for unity. Do you agree?"

"Of course," Roy said.

Ronny said, "Supervisor Chu, Dorn and I are

trouble shooters. We're widely experienced in interplanetary difficulties. I'm the leader of the group. I suggest you make me temporary chief of our whole number."

Rosemary said, "I nominate Ronny to be our temporary head, in charge of whatever action we can take."

"Second," David said.

Rosemary said, "Are there any more nominations?"

There were none.

"All in favor say, 'Aye.'"

All said aye, including Lee Chang and Dorn, who seemed slightly amused at this show of the democratic method.

Ronny said, "Wizard. Just before you four entered, Rosemary was giving us a run-down on your experiences here with the Dawnmen. You've been here something like a week. Have you any indication what they expect to do with us? The Brahmin who communicated with us merely said that we were to be turned over to the Kshatriyas, the soldier ants, as Rosemary called them, for their annual ceremonies."

The five from Einstein looked at him. "You don't know what the annual ceremonies are?" Roy said.

"No. Do you?"

Roy said, "They evidently come down from the antiquity of the Dawnmen. The Holy Ultimate only knows how long ago it was that they were so primitive a people. The annual ceremonies of the Kshatriyas amount to gladiator fights. Each young Kshatriyas must prove himself in the arena before he enters into full . . . full manhood, I suppose you'd call it."

18

"What the hell's that got to do with us?" Ronny said. "We're not even Dawnmen, not to mention belonging to the Kshatriya caste."

Gil said, "It seems that in ancient times, on the world where they first evolved. and before they spread out over other planets as well, they had a society somewhat similar to that of ancient Earth. That is, they were split up into different tribes and nations. When they captured enemies in battle they were sent to the arena. If they survived, they were turned free."

Roy added, "Though they no longer have wars, in the old sense, the tradition is still with them. It's part of their rituals, even though megayears have gone by since then. Last time, they warned you and Wyler off, but this time they are taking few chances of our returning and informing other strangers of the location of the Dawnworlds. This time, we fight for our lives."

Dorn said, "With what weapons?"

Gil said, "If I understand it, with the ancient weapons of their... people. If you can call the Dawnmen people."

Ronny said, "What are their ancient weapons?"

Charles said, "We don't know that. The only weapon we've seen is a three-headed spear. Unless the swagger stick of the captain of the squad that arrested us is really some sort of a weapon."

"If it is," Dorn said, "it's hardly an ancient one." He looked at Ronny. "Have you been checked out on swords?"

"Swords? No," Ronny said. "Why do you think that they'd have swords?"

Dorn said, "It occurs to me that any humanoid type life form would evolve very similar weapons. The war club, at first, then the knife and spear. When metals were developed the sword would appear, as it did on Earth from Japan to England. Even the Aztecs had a type of sword which used razor-sharp obsidian chips set into a wooden blade."

"Well," Ronny said, "even if that's what they use for their gladiator fights, it won't effect me much. I've never had any kind of sword in my hand in my life."

"Neither have I," Dorn said. He looked at the four men from Einstein.

They all shook their heads. Roy said, "I've never had any kind of weapon in my hands."

And Gil said, "Nor have I."

David said, "Charles and I had pistols when we arrived. I brought them from Avalon, after a scientific conference I attended there. But they didn't work when we tried to defend ourselves from the Dawnmen."

"Oh, wizard," Ronny said in disgust. "Out of the lot of us, no one knows anything about the use of primitive weapons. And you can trust the Holy Ultimate that our Kshatriya friends are trained with them from earliest youth. They'll all be experts."

"Well," Dorn said, "I did some boxing when I was in school. I made the university championship."

173

"That's better than nothing," Ronny said. "I used to practice judo as a hobby back before I joined Section G. I'm more than a little rusty by now, I suppose." He looked at the other four.

They all shook their heads and Gil said, "On Einstein, we don't indulge in sports involving violence."

Lee Chang Chu said, "I know kenpo."

Rosemary said, "What's kenpo?"

"An early Chinese form of karate."

"What's karate?"

"A method of fighting with your hands and feet," the Chinese girl said.

Rosemary looked at her wanly. "It doesn't make any difference. The ritual of the annual ceremonies doesn't provide for women fighting. For all I know, perhaps the Dawnwomen are liberated now, but they weren't in the primitive times of the race. So the rituals have no place for women."

"What's to happen to us, then?" Lee Chang said.

Rosemary shrugged and said, "We're to be sacrificed on the altar on top of the pyramid in their sacred complex, following the games. We won't be alone. All the Kshatriyas who survive the games but have failed to triumph are also sacrificed."

Roy said bitterly, "Evidently it was the system, in the old days of weeding out incompetent warriors. Each year the boys who had reached the age to become full warriors fought it out in the arena. Those that triumphed became members of the army, the half that didn't either died in the arena, or were sacrificed later."

"As you can see," Gil added, "after a few million years you'd wind up with a pretty tough warrior caste."

Dorn said apologetically to Lee Chang and Rosemary, "I doubt if our fates will be much different than your own. As Ronny said, the Kshatriyas will be experts in the use of their weapons and none of us have even seen one, not to speak of knowing how to handle them."

They mulled it over some more, but there was little else to be said.

Ronny and Dorn questioned them on the possibilities of escape but the other four men claimed it was utterly impossible. They had explored every aspect of getting out of the house and had come up with a blank. Besides, what if they did escape? Where could they go that the Dawnmen wouldn't find them? Even their spaceship was inoperative.

Ronny said, "We could call down the *Alexander Hamilton* and have them pick us up."

"If they could nullify our spacecraft, I assume they could do the same to yours," one of the others told him.

"When do the annual ceremonies begin?" Dorn asked.

Rosemary said, "We don't know."

She was far from the smiling, bright Rosemary that the Section G agents had first met on Einstein. On the face of it, she had been under pressure long enough for her defenses to have collapsed. She was obviously in a state of despair.

Ronny frowned and said to her, "What are you doing here, anyway? I thought from what Marvin said back on Einstein that you were sending a delegation of your highest intelligences for this romp. You told us you were comparatively stupid."

"That was a fake," she sighed. "We wanted to put

175

one of our number in a position to set you up. I was chosen."

Following their conference, the three Section G agents were given a conducted tour of the premises. The rest of the building bore out what they had found in the living room. It was simple, to the point of being stark, but the furniture was comfortable. The bathrooms were surprisingly similar to those of Earth settled worlds, but, once again, Ronny decided, a humanoid life form would eventually come up with approximately the same toilet equipment; the bathtub, the shower, the flush toilet.

The dining room was something of a mystery, however. The Einstein five had never figured out how it worked. Periodically, the legless, anti-gravity dining room table would disappear. In moments, it would become visible again, bearing sufficient food for the number of persons present. None of them were particularly happy with the strange food, but it obviously supported their life form. Rosemary hated it and would eat only enough to keep her going.

The bedrooms were, once more, stark, and with no facilities for storing clothes. It occurred to Ronny that the Dawnmen had no need to store clothes. With a matter conversion unit, and he assumed that each dwelling had one, you could make*new clothing, or anything else you might wish, at any time.

The beds were about half as high as the Earthlings were used to, but quite comfortable. There were no covers whatsoever, not even a bedsheet. One slept on the equivalent of a mattress which seemed similar to a water-mattress, though filled with something other than water. They never did find out what.

176

Each room had one or more large windows, according to its size, and they could look out without difficulty over the fabulous countryside. It was difficult to realize that from the exterior the house was invisible and all in it. Only by opening the front door could it be seen that a dwelling was here.

The building was fairly large, with five bedrooms in all, each with two beds. To accommodate the newcomers, those from Einstein did some switching about. Lee Chang and Ronny took over one room, Dorn another. Rosemary had made a wry mouth when it became obvious that Ronny was to sleep with the Chinese girl. However, Ronny suspected that she was probably not sleeping alone, but with one, or possibly more, of the Einstein men. He rather doubted that Rosemary slept alone very often, not with the sexual mores under which she had been raised.

The inspection of the premises over, they retired again to the living room. Ronny pulled up a chair before the floating table top and brought forth his communicator. He had his fingers mentally crossed. In view of what Rosemary had said about their time instruments being disrupted, all he needed was for his Section G communicator not to function. He was relieved to get an answer when he called the *Alexander Hamilton.*

Ronny reported briefly to John Fodor, who looked worried, but obviously knew that there was nothing that he could do. Thus far, he hadn't spotted any signs of Dawnworld spacecraft, which could only be a relief to him.

Ronny told him that there was no night and day here and that evidently you slept when you became tired. He was beginning to feel that way already, so if he didn't report in within the next six hours, the captain was not to become alarmed. He would as soon as sleep was over.

The captain gone, Ronny called the Octagon on Earth again and was put through to Sid Jakes. He gave him the whole story.

"A gladiator fight?" the assistant to Ross Metaxa protested. "The more I hear about these Dawnmen, the more I disbelieve. How can they be that far advanced and still put up with gladiator fights?"

Ronny shook his head. "They live by traditions and rituals, most of them going back to the dawn of their race. They're bred into them. Evidently, it's impossible to change them, any more than it's possible to change a drone into a worker bee."

"So the story is that if you win, you go free. All but Lee Chang, that is, and the girl from Einstein."

"That's right, Sid," Ronny said lowly.

"Well, you and Dorn take the cloddies, Ronny, and figure out some way of getting the girls off the hook, especially Lee Chang."

"Ha, you dreamer," Ronny growled at him.

"Stiff upper lip, old chappie," Sid Jakes grinned at him. "You'll find some way. You always do."

"Having a wonderful time," Ronny snarled at him. "Wish you were here . . . instead."

He flicked the communicator off and turned back to Dorn and Lee Chang who had been following the reports he had been making.

He snarled, "That grinning funker."

But Lee Chang shook her head. "Poor Sid's worried sick. How would you like to be in his position, sitting helpless there in Greater Washington?"

Gil entered and said, "Meal time again. At least the table is freshly loaded with their Dawnworld gook."

They followed him into the dining room where the others had already gathered and found that Rosemary had exaggerated the quality of the food. It wasn't as bad as all that. They were accustomed to none of the basics but they were obviously nourishing. There were even some fruits for dessert that were quite exotic in taste, though less sweet than the Earthlings were used to.

Following the meal, the three Section G agents felt like sleep. They were still used to the routine of the *Alexander Hamilton* in spite of the daylight that prevailed on the Dawnworld. The others had fallen into the habit of sleeping when tired, no matter how many hours they had been up.

Lee Chang and Ronny retired to their room. There were two windows and they could discover no way of darkening them. There were no drapes or blinds and evidently no mechanical means of opaquing them. It would seem that the Dawnworlders slept in bright daylight. Ronny vaguely wondered if this perpetual light had always been so, or if it was a result of planetary engineering, perhaps some megayears ago. In either case, the need for dark to sleep comfortably would have evolved out of the Dawnmen, if they ever had it.

He wasn't up to sex, even if Lee Chang had been. The fact that she was doomed, even if he had a very remote chance of surviving, hung heavily over the two of them. They undressed, kissed, and took to separate beds.

She said, before they dropped off into sleep, "Ronny, during your years as a Section G operative, have you ever before been in a spot where it seemed impossible that you could survive?"

"Yes," he said.

After a moment, she said, "So have I, but never one where it seemed so very impossible."

There was no answer to that.

When they awakened, they made their toilets, dressed and returned to the living room to find nobody but Gil there. Gil and the dogs. Boy and Plotz had elected to spend their time here, rather than in the smaller bedrooms.

Boy looked up and said, "Boss, when do we eat? There's a big spread on the dining room table."

"I suppose now," Ronny told him. "Eat, drink and be merry for . . ." He broke it off. It wasn't funny, with Lee Chang there beside him. And, seated across the room, Gil, who had never been in physical combat in his life and was slated to go up against expert gladiators.

Lee Chang looked at him from the side of her almond eyes but she had the guts to be amused. She said softly, in her Lee Chang voice, "You've got a real touch there, darling."

"Sorry," he said gruffly. They headed for the dining room.

Dorn was already there and making himself up a plate of the unappetizing looking Dawnworld dishes.

He said, pushing his glasses higher on the bridge of his nose, "I am of the opinion that we should act on the basis that our best bet is to keep up our strengths—we'll need them."

The Dawnmen didn't have the institution of different dishes for different times of the day. The

180

food presented at this meal was identical to that Ronny had eaten at the last one. The bee-hive culture, Ronny thought inwardly. But he heaped his plate, following Dorn's advice.

That worthy looked at Lee Chang thoughtfully. He said, "My dear, I am a physician, among other things. I could kill you quickly and almost painlessly, in seconds."

Lee Chang looked at him and made an Oriental moue. She said, "Thanks, Dorn. But, no thanks. I follow the old saying, as long as there's life, there's hope. Besides, as I told you, I know kenpo. If at all possible, I'm going to get in at least one deadly blow at these funkers."

"Well said," Dorn rumbled. He turned back to his food, his face somewhat embarrassed.

Ronny had put down two plates for the dogs.

Boy chomped and said, "This stuff is grim. Don't they have meat on this planet?"

Ronny said, "It would seem not. They don't even seem to have animal life at all. That captain, or whatever he was, of the Kshatriyas, not only didn't know what a pet was, but obviously had trouble in his telepathy in using the thought animal."

"Some world," Boy growled, but he went back to his food.

Roy wandered in, yawning, and began to fill a plate. He said, "I wish that they at least supplied us with reading material, or some games, or something. I'm beginning to go around the bend from sheer boredom."

But it was then that a thought came into all of their minds.

Prepare to receive us.

181

19

They filed back into the living room and found the others there.

Gil said unhappily, "This is the first we've seen of any of them since they stuck us in here. I have a sneaking suspicion that the time has come for the annual ceremonies."

The door opened and through it, swagger stick in hand, strode the Kshatriya officer, followed by two of his trident-bearing soldiers.

He faced them and the thought came, *It is time for you to choose your weapons.*

"Well, at least we've got a choice," Ronny muttered.

The two soldiers posted themselves near the door, which had automatically closed. The officer approached the large center table, floating there without support and looked at its surface. The table disappeared, to reappear almost immediately covered with a wide range of weapons—hand weapons.

Ronny had never seen such a variety outside the museum in Greater Washington. Possibly half of them were unknown to the Earthlings, even from books. The rest resembled, in varying degrees, early weapons of Earth, some of them so primitive that it was difficult to believe that they would still be in use. There was even what was obviously a throwing stick, quite similar to a boomerang. There were spears in variety ranging from a flint-tipped throwing spear to metal-tipped javelins and pikes. There were various types of clubs, including a mace with a vicious-looking flanged metal head. There were swords of a dozen varieties, one even with a double blade looking as though it would make a clumsy weapon.

The six Earthlings looked down at the display in dismay. The collection looked terrible businesslike, and unlikely.

Each of you is allowed to choose two weapons for the fray.

Ronny looked at the four men from Einstein. He said, "I suggest that you each choose a short spear, one of these metal tipped ones about six feet long. You'll use it for jabbing in protecting yourselves, rather than throwing. And a short sword, one of those that look Roman. None of you know fencing, but those have both points and double cutting edges. You can just flail away."

The four nodded dumbly and each in turn pointed out to the Kshatriya officer their choice.

Dorn, meanwhile, had taken up the largest of the swords, which looked considerably like a double handed Viking weapon of the Dark Ages of Earth. It was obviously meant to be used gripped with two hands, since its weight precluded an ordinary man from wielding it. But Dorn swung it back and forth singlehandedly with ease, his face thoughtful.

Ronny took up a heavy short spear of the type once known on Earth as a boar spear and considered it.

Boy looked at him and said, "How about me, Boss?"

Ronny looked down at him and frowned, "How do you mean, Boy?"

Boy hung out his tongue, gave a couple of pants and said, "We Vizslas were originally war dogs. For two thousand years or more we fought side by side with the Huns on their way from Siberia to where they finally settled down around Budapest. We're not this size for nothing and we don't have the speed we have for nothing. The Magyars, the Huns, raised us basically as war dogs."

Ronny stared at him. The Dawnworld Kshatriyas had never seen animals, evidently, not to speak of war dogs.

He turned to the Dawnman officer and said, "What are the rules pertaining to weapons that can be utilized in the arena?"

Any weapon can be utilized that predates powered projectiles.

"Very well, I demand the right to utilize a weapon of my own planet that predates projectiles."

The Kshatriya scowled at him. *What weapon? You brought no weapons with you.* He evidently hadn't taken in what Boy had said.

"A Magyar war dog."

"What is a Magyar war dog?"

Ronny pointed at Boy.

The other's face went blank for a moment. Then a new voice entered into the minds of the Earthlings. It was that of the Brahmin.

I have read your mind and memory and the information behind what you have said is correct. In the early days of Earth, men fought accompanied by their war dogs. Your request is acceptable. You shall be allowed the war dog and one other weapon.

Plotz looked up at Dorn and said, "Cut me a piece

184

of the steak. I don't like the smell of these people. In fact, they don't have a smell. Dogs go by smells, and I like you but not them."

Dorn had on his own come to the same conclusion as Ronny had. "All right," he said. He turned to the officer. "I'll take this sword and the female war dog."

Ronny decided on his boar spear.

All the weapons were returned to the table which disappeared, to return almost immediately with four short spears, four short swords, Ronny's boar spear and Dorn's Viking-like double handed sword. The six men took them up and turned to look at the Kshatriya.

Follow me, he said in their minds and headed for one of the walls.

They eyed him in puzzlement, but fell in behind.
The women will remain here.

The two soldiers who had been posted at the door followed after.

Just before the officer reached the wall, an apperture opened in it and he marched through. The Earthlings followed along with the dogs and the two soldiers behind them.

Rosemary called out in a choked voice, "Good luck, boys."

Lee Chang looked after them wordlessly. The four Einstein men, in particular, hardly knew how to carry their weapons.

They emerged into what had every appearance of a medieval dungeon, a sizeable dungeon of crudely worked stone, a type of granite, by the looks of it. The dungeon was completely unfurnished. It was a far cry from the house they had just left. The room was out of the furthest past.

Gil looked blankly back at the now closed entry

through which they had just passed. It had closed again, leaving no signs. The wall was of the same stone as the balance of the room. He said, "They've mastered how to go through under-space bodily. Instant transportation from one place to another, probably any distance."

Nobody bothered to answer him.

Roy was looking pale about the gills. He said, "I think that I'm going to be sick."

Ronny stepped up quickly and slapped his face. "Snap out of it," he snarled. "You got yourself into this. We're going to have to fight as a team. We need every man..." he looked down at the two grim Vizslas, "...and dog."

Roy shook his head and looked embarrassed and had the courage to say, "Sorry. I'll do my best."

At the far side of the dungeon was a window barred with what looked like iron rods.

The officer gestured at it. *The Arena,* he thought at them.

The six Earthlings went over and stared out.

They looked upon an arena which resembled one of the early Roman ones, perhaps the Collosseum. The floor of it was strewn with sand. The only difference was that there were no observers in the stands, which were delapidated and looked as though no one had been seated in them for long millenea. It would seem that the Dawnworld people did not watch the gladiator battles. At least, not in person. Ronny suspected that there were the equivalent of Tri-Di lenses directed on the arena floor.

Even as they watched, waiting for whatever was to

come, heavy wooden doors opened on the opposite side and long rows of Dawnmen filed in, marching in perfect step.

They moved about in unison, taking positions that had obviously been previously set. The variety of weapons they carried was not extensive. It would seem that although a wide selection was offered, a few were preferred. The trident was prominent among them. So were various other types of spears. And most had, as an auxiliary weapon, some type of sword. Ronny could see none who carried a boomerang, though there were some who had heavy maces, rather than swords.

The officer's voice came into their minds. *The first stage of the annual ceremonies will be conducted by aspiring members of the Kshatriya. Similar contests are being held throughout the planet and on every other planet of the ... Dawnworlds. From among the survivors who have in particular triumphed, will be selected six who will have the honor of killing you.*

"God damned savages," David muttered.

The gladiators flourished their weapons.

"We who are about to die, salute you," Dorn Horsten murmured.

And suddenly the arena erupted into chaos.

"Watch carefully," Ronny rapped. "We aren't going to have much time to study their fighting methods, but you could pick up some ideas that might save your life later."

Roy looked pale about the gills again, as the first Dawnman went down, a javelin through his belly and coming out his back. It was only seconds later

187

that a trident man impaled a sword-wielding opponent, who survived long enough to completely sever his killer's head from his trunk.

Ronny was breathing deeply, even as he watched. Every man out there was handling his weapons like a veteran, with a skill denoting long years of drill. This was even worse that he had expected. They were *all* experts.

They invariably fought one against one, not in teams. When a gladiator downed his immediate opponent, he turned to find another. Wounded men were mercilessly cut down, but once prone on the sands they were not finished off. Being reserved for the sacrificial altar, Ronny thought grimly. Indeed, red-kilted stretcher bearers began to appear and pick up the fallen wounded. The dead they let lie.

Ronny was sorry now that he hadn't chosen a trident, rather than his boar spear. It was obviously one of the most efficient and vicious weapons in the arena, and highly preferred by the Dawnmen. The prongs were razor sharp and could be used for slashing as well as prodding.

In surprisingly short order, approximately half of the young fighting Dawnmen were on the sands, dead, bleeding to death, or being picked up by the stretcher bearers. It occurred to him now that these latter were not Kshatriya but members of the Sudras caste, the working caste that he had come in contact with the first time he had been on this Dawnworld. They moved about, carrying their stretchers, cheerfully, smilingly, all as though this was a daily affair. Ronny shuddered.

Suddenly, some sort of signal must have been sounded, telepathically, undoubtedly. For the still-standing fighters came to a halt, held high their weapons and began to file toward the wooden doors through which they had entered. Half a dozen of those sprawled on the sands tried to crawl after them and were rejected at the gates by guards.

They aren't all as much ant-men as all that, Ronny thought, compassion in him in spite of his position. The crawlers were scheduled for the altar.

As soon as the gladiators had filed out, members of the Sudras caste hurried in and began to sweep the sands of the arena, covering over the blood and sometimes the guts. Others went about dragging off the corpses.

"Okay," Ronny said. "Now comes the moment of truth. Now listen to me, and carefully. They fight as individuals, man against man. We cooperate. I assume that you've all read about the phalanx, in Earth history."

"I haven't," Charles said. "I'm a physicist."

Ronny groaned. "No time to explain," he said. "But we fight as a unit. Roy, David, Gil, Charles, you're our center. Stick your swords in your belts. Go in with the spears advanced, held in both hands, side by side. Grab the swords out later, when needed. But initially you go in with the spears advanced. Dorn will be on your right flank with that overgrown cheese knife he selected. He'll be further off than I'll be because he'll need lots of room to swing that confounded thing. Plotz will be to his right, doing whatever it is that war dogs do."

He looked around at them. "I'll be on the left flank with Boy." He took a deep breath. "We're going to take casualties. These opponents are well trained. You might say that they've been professionals for a few megayears. There'll be the four of you, side by side, with Dorn and I and the dogs on each end. If one of you falls, close up ranks. We continue to fight as a unit, as long as two or more of us are standing."

"I'm going to be sick," Roy said, his face green.

"Shut up," Ronny told him. "And now listen. We have to go in there projecting confidence and high morale. Our battle shout will be . . ." he thought for a moment ". . . *United Planets Forever*, and we'll flourish our weapons as we shout it."

"Oh, come now," Dorn said, "can't you think of something a bit more, ah, inspiring?"

Ronny glared at him and growled, "I don't have the time. Do you want to write a sonnet?"

"Shakespearean or Spenserian?" Dorn said, smiling one of his seldom smiles.

Ronny appreciated his attempt at morale building humor but turned back to the four from Einstein and said, "There's small chance that we'll get out of this and actually there's precious little we're fighting for besides our lives. These Dawnworld people could take United Planets inbetween scratches of a mosquito bite . . . if they had mosquitos. However, there is a certain dignity, embracing our whole race, in our going down . . . like men."

"Hear, hear," Dorn Horsten said sarcastically.

"Screw you, Dorn," Ronny grinned at him.

Dorn said, "Shouldn't you report to John Fodor? I think he must be getting anxious."

Ronny said, "Damn little good it will do us," but he complied and got out his communicator.

When Captain Fodor's face faded in, anxious, Ronny rapped, "We're about to go into a gladiator

190

fiasco. If I don't report back to you, in the next couple of hours, or if one of the others don't, in case I go down, make a bee-line for Earth—if you can make it. Our chances of survival are practically nil."

"Should we land and attempt to come to your assistance?"

"Don't be a cloddy." Ronny flicked off the instrument.

He turned back to the others. Boy and Plotz had been standing on their back feet, their paws on the window sill, and looking out.

Boy said, "I still say, I'd like to get my chompers into one of those bare legs."

20

You will prepare yourselves to enter the arena, the voice that came into their minds said.

The two foot soldiers manually opened the heavy wooden door that led out into the arena and the six Earthlings, followed by the dogs, filed out. Simultaneously, a door on the opposite side of the arena opened and six Dawnmen came running through.

Ronny said, "All right, get in line as I told you. We'll wait for them here, with the wall behind us, so they won't be able to get to our rear. Besides that, they've already been fighting and are a little tired. Plodding through the sand to come at us will increase that."

"Good thinking," Dorn called over to him.

The Dawnmen, seeing that the Earthlings were waiting for them to take the initiative, formed a straight line of their own and broke into a trot.

Gil said bitterly, "Maybe they fight as individuals when fighting against each other, but they're a team now."

That wasn't the only thing that went wrong in Ronny's calculations.

The whole thing lasted a few minutes.

Charles was the first to go down. While still some ten meters off, one of the Dawnmen came to a sudden halt, threw back his arm and heaved he javelin he carried.

"Look out!" Ronny barked.

But too late, the Einstein man shrieked and went down, completely transfixed through the solar plexus area.

The javelin thrower drew his sword and came on again, heading for Ronny. All of a sudden the Section G agent had no more time to observe his comrades. He advanced his boar spear cautiously, as the other came in to the attack. The spear was primarily a defensive weapon, while the sword was offensive.

He prodded and was confounded by the reflexes of his opponent. The other jumped back, hacked quickly and splintered the end of Ronny's spear so that its iron tip broke off and fell to the ground.

But it was then that Boy came in, running low and fast and snarling. He sped around the startled Dawnman and grabbed him by the naked calf of his right leg and ripped savagely, tearing the fleshy calf completely away. The Dawnman swung his sword down cutting the dog across the back.

The diversion gave Ronny his opportunity. He stepped in quickly and ran the splintered end of his boar spear into the other's belly. The warrior fell, taking the broken spear with him. Ronny stooped down and grabbed up the other's sword. He shot an agonized look at Boy who was down on the sand panting in agony.

He had no time for the dog. He spun and reentered the fray, sword in hand.

Of the four from Einstein, only Roy was still on his feet and even he had obviously taken a blow or two. He was jabbing at one of the Dawnmen with his spear, desperately.

But it was Dorn who won the day. Dorn and Plotz. The big man, his pince-nez glasses firmly on the bridge of his nose, was swinging his gigantic sword like a madman, flailing away like a windmill, gone berserk. His very lack of finesse, his ignorance of every principle of swordsmanship, was his greatest advantage. The others were highly trained, even instinctively trained, to know that for each blow there was a parry and a counterblow. Swordsmanship is an art, a very highly honed art.

It was no art the way Doctor Dorn Horsten played it. It was mayhem. His sword had three times the weight of any of theirs and Dorn Horsten had at least three times the strength of any of them.

But Plotz was the ultimate factor.

As members of the Kshatriya caste, they were warriors born. For megayears fighting had been bred into them. They practiced with every weapons known and they excelled in them. But none had ever seen a dog, much less a Magyar war dog. Plotz too had her fighting instincts, bred into her race a double thousand years and more.

Snarling, her mouth slavering, her canine teeth gleaming white, she zipped around among them, behind them, sometimes right between their legs to upset them. She was astonishingly fast, considering her heavy-set body. One went down in a ludicrous pratt-fall, and she had ripped out his throat almost before he hit the sand.

Roy fell from the blow of a mace but gave Ronny the time to finish off his killer with a sword thrust into his kidneys. Ronny was probably the most experienced of the Earthlings so far as personal, hand to hand combat, was concerned. His judo hobby was now paying off. Not that he was able to practice it—cold steel was involved now—but his reflexes were good, and he was able to think fast in action.

But it was Dorn and Plotz who won the day.

And suddenly there were no more Dawnmen on their feet, save one who was staggering, a hand to his throat, blood spurting from a severed artery. He wouldn't stand long, as his life ebbed away, ebbed away.

Dorn dropped his sword and quickly went over to the four inept fallen men from Einstein. One by one, he checked them.

Ronny was down on his knees beside Boy, who looked up at him and tried to wag his tail. It didn't come off.

He panted, "Sorry I didn't last very long, Boss. I can't move my back legs."

Ronny closed his eyes in agony. The dog's spine was severed.

He said, "Dorn's a doctor. He'll fix you up."

Boy lolled his tongue from the side of his mouth and said, his voice losing strength even as he talked, "He doesn't even have his little black bag and I suspect that vet materials are in short supply on this planet."

Plotz was looking down on him. She said, woefully, "Boy, I'm sorry I was so mean to you."

He looked at her and his lips thinned back over his teeth as though he was trying to smile. "You weren't mean to me, Puppy. Name one of the litter after me."

Dorn came up. He said to Ronny, his shoulders slumping, "They're all dead."

"So is Boy," Plotz said, her voice so low as hardly to be heard.

A voice in their heads said, *"You will return to the*

room from which you departed.

Ronny came to his feet. "Okay, you Dawnman bastard," he said, looking down one last time at his dog, the animal who had saved his life.

They returned to the dungeon-like room where they had left the Kshatriya officer and his two men.

The Kshatriyas looked thunderstruck. It was the first time that any of them had depicted expression on their faces. They had expected the Earthlings to go down to a man before the onslaught of their Dawnman opponents. The officer looked at Plotz with profound respect.

She snarled at him, "I'd call you a son-of-a-bitch, but I wouldn't insult my species."

This way, the voice in their heads said and the officer led to the point where the aperature had allowed them to enter.

The strange doorway opened again and they passed through to the living room where they had left Lee Chang and Rosemary such a short time ago, but so long ago.

The two women had been seated, misery on their faces, but they shot instantly erect, their eyes in relief.

Lee Chang blurted, "You made it!"

Rosemary said, "But where are the others?"

Dorn shook his head sadly at her. "My dear, they are dead."

"All four of them; Roy, David, Gil, Charles?" She was aghast.

Ronny said, "They fought like ... men. But they were inexperienced, Rosemary. Boy's dead, too. He went down saving my life."

"I see," Rosemary said, and slumped back into

196

her chair. "And I'll go next. Lee Chang and I."

The Kshatriyas officer took one last admiring look at Plotz and, followed by his two men, went to the front door of the building. It opened automatically and they left.

Lee Chang said, "What happened?"

Ronny slumped down on the couch, feeling exhaustion in spite of the brief period of the action. He said, "We fought six of them. The dogs threw them off balance. Dorn and I, and Plotz, survived."

The voice of the one they identified as a Brahmin came to them in their minds. It said: *Ronald Bronston, Dorn Horsten, Plotz—you have triumphed in the arena. By our traditions, you are free to leave. Reassure yourselves; the planets of your origin are not endangered by us, since you have won survival, and if we destroyed them, we would destroy you as well. However, in the future if other representatives of your race attempt to land on one of our worlds, the spacecraft carrying them will be destroyed and all occupants.*

Ronny said grimly, "Thanks. What about Lee Chang Chu and Rosemary?"

By our traditions, they must be sacrificed on the Sacred Altar Stone. There is no traditional means by which they can redeem themselves.

Rosemary moaned.

The voice went on: *We were astonished by your success. We assumed, particularly in view of the fact that you were not acquainted with the weapons of the Kshatriya caste, that you would die in the arena and the problem of your knowing of the location of our worlds would die with you. We then planned to destroy the spacecraft you have in orbit about this planet. But now you have won your freedom and hence the spacecraft cannot be destroyed or you would have no means of leaving us. We have been highly impressed by the conduct of your war dogs, and particularly Plotz, who confounded our Kshatriyas.*

A quick inspiration came to Ronny Bronston. He said, "She is yours."

We do not understand.

"By tradition, on the planet of her birth, Einstein, if one admires a possession, the owner gives it to him."

There was a long silence. Finally the telepathic voice said, *Probing your mind tells us that what you have said is true. We are a race that is fully aware of the importance of tradition. We accept the gift.*

"Hey," Plotz said in protest. "Are you humans selling me down the river?"

The Brahmin's voice said, *A gift for a gift, Ronald Bronston, it is one of our own traditions. What do you request?*

Ronny said evenly, "The lives of our two women."

Lee Chang said quickly, "Wait a minute, Ronny. The matter converter, or the anti-gravity. They'd revolutionize technology in United Planets. We're only two persons. This involves billions of people."

Ronny shook his head. "What the Brahmin told Rosemary and her colleagues was correct. The human race isn't ready as yet for matter converters, anti-gravity, personal travel through under-space, and so forth. When we're ready, we'll discover them. It's the old story. When there was a need, in turn, for the steamship, the railroad, the automobile, the airplane, the spaceship, they were discovered."

198

Correct, the mind-voice said. *And now you are free to leave.*

Ronny nodded wearily and said, "The dog is pregnant. She will have young. You will be able to reproduce her species indefinitely."

Yes. We are aware of this. And now, farewell.

The mental presence was suddenly gone. How they knew, they couldn't know. But it was gone.

Ronny looked at Plotz. He said, "I don't know if I'm sorry or not. It became instantly clear when the Brahmin admired you—and Boy—that if I presented you to him, he would be obligated to give something in return. It was the one way to save Lee Chang and Rosemary."

The dog put out her tongue and gave a few quick pants and said, "Yes, I've figured that out by now and I agree. Besides, it's not as bad as all that. My pups..." she hesitated a moment before adding, "and Boy's, will spread all over these worlds. We're the equivalents of Adam and Eve—in a canine sort of way. Who knows what the future holds? I heard you explaining once that these Dawnworlders aren't really intelligent. All they've got is accumulated knowledge. Well, we Einstein Vizslas are smart." She hesitated a moment and then added, "Besides, we're Magyar war dogs and they killed Boy."

"Holy Ultimate," Dorn said.

A door opened and Boy walked in, an elaborate bandage on his back and looking exhausted.

"Hello, everybody," he said, and slumped down. They ogled him.

"You're dead!" Ronny blurted. "That man severed your spine."

"Don't write me off so easy, Boss," Boy panted. "I

199

was dead for only a few minutes. They liked my style, so they went to work on me. I guess they've got pretty advanced medicine."

Rosemary blurted, "But Gil, Roy, David, Charles..."

Boy looked at her. "Sorry," he said. "I guess the Dawnmen didn't like their style." He gave a weary double pant. "As a matter of fact, it was pretty bad. I watched the whole thing after I took my hit. Plotz and the Boss and Dorn were the only ones that counted."

Aftermath

Ronny didn't get in touch with the Octagon, to report, until after they had returned to the *Alexander Hamilton* and to a relieved Captain John Fodor. There hadn't been any difficulty. The five of them, including Boy, had taken their leave of Plotz and left the house, the door of which had automatically opened. Dorn carried Boy. They had walked about a half kilometer and then Ronny raised the space cruiser with his communicator and called for that craft's skipper to pick them up.

As soon as they were in space, Lee Chang went to her cabin, secured her star chart, still sealed, and returned with it to the bridge. As before, the officers and crew on watch were dismissed and she set the course for a return to Earth.

Afterwards, she and Ronny went to the ship's officer's mess and rejoined the others.

Ronny looked at Rosemary and Lee Chang and said, "Well, now there are three of us that know the navigational coordinates of the Dawnworlds. That's three too many."

But Rosemary shook her head. "I don't. Gil and Roy were the navigators. I don't know anything about navigation."

Ronny said thoughtfully, "Is there anybody else, back on Einstein that knows the coordinates?"

"Not that I know of."

"Wizard. I'd better get in touch with the Old Man." He brought out his communicator and went through the usual routine. Ross Metaxa was again not available, so Sid Jakes faded in.

He grinned. "Still with us, eh? I told you that you'd make it."

Ronny looked at him sarcastically. "Mission accomplished. We had to fight it out in an arena for our freedom. The four men from Einstein were killed. Dorn and I survived and were able to make a deal with the Brahmin who communicated with us, for Lee Chang and Rosemary. We also were told that the next time a human ship landed on a Dawnworld it would be destroyed. I'll give you more details when I get back. Meanwhile, I resign. I'm going to join a nunnery. It's a safer way of making a living."

Sid Jakes ignored the latter. "Great," he said. "How'd the new agent work out?"

"What new agent?"

Sid Jakes scowled at him and said, "Why the one you reported recruiting on Einstein. Buoy, or something like that."

"Oh," Ronny said vaguely. "He worked out fine. He saved my life in the fight."

"Wizard," the other said. "Make him a probationary agent. And we'll put him through the Section G courses when you get back." His face faded from the communicator screen.

Ronny turned and looked at Boy, who gave him the old double wag of the bobbed tail, and said, "Would you like to be a Section G agent?"

Lee Chang and Dorn had been laughing but Lee Chang knocked it off and stared at Ronny. She said,

202

"Have you gone drivel-happy? As an agent of supervisor rank you are impowered to recruit new agents, but I doubt that Sid realizes that Boy is a dog."

Ronny said, "There's nothing in the United Planets Charter that says all member worlds must be humanity settled. Suppose, as we expand into the galaxy, we run into an intelligent alien life form that is compatible. Suppose they join United Planets. Wouldn't their race be eligible to join the Bureau of Investigation?"

She looked at him blankly. "Why...I suppose so."

"Wizard. Boy is an intelligent life form. His cover is perfect. I can think of a dozen circumstances where his services would be priceless. Think what a spy he'd make."

Boy said, "I don't know. I kind of like dogging for a living. It's not a bad life at all. No responsibility, pretty good chow, and a lot of laughs. Would you still be my Boss?"

"Well, I'm supervisor rank, as Lee Chang is. We'd both be your bosses, in a way."

Boy thought about it. "What's in it for me?" he said finally.

"Why, you'd get a salary, just like anybody else. You'd start at five hundred interplanetary credits a month. That's a hell of a lot of money for a dog. You could buy any kind of food you wanted." Ronny snorted. "For that matter, you could buy yourself a whole kennel full of female Vizslas. Have a regular harem."

"Hmmm," Boy said. "At first it sounds great, but at second thought I wonder if I'd like a bunch of dumb bitches around all the time."

"You could rent a special seraglio for them and only spend as much time as you wanted. The pay is high. You'd be able to afford to hire a full time attendant for the harem. The equivalent of a eunuch."

Boy thought about it. He gave his tail a wag or so. "Hmmm, and I'd be this human attendant's boss, eh?"

"Of course."

Boy shook his head in wonder. "I've heard the old wheeze about when man bites dog, it's news. But this is really news. Dog hires man."

www.ingramcontent.com/pod-product-compliance
Lightning Source LLC
Chambersburg PA
CBHW030322180626
46810CB00003B/1192